T0064065

SUN NEVER RISES

SUN NEVER RISES

ANI TOM MARIA

PARTRIDGE
A Penguin Random House Company

ISBN: Hardcover   978-1-4828-4344-6
               Softcover   978-1-4828-4343-9
               eBook   978-1-4828-4345-3

To order additional copies of this book, contact
Partridge India
000 800 10062 62
orders.india@partridgepublishing.com

www.partridgepublishing.com/india

Contents

You Too, Eva

Washington DC

President Abraham Lincoln has amended Thirteenth Bill to abolish slavery in the House of Commons. Amid hue and cry, the historical bill has been passed by the representatives of House of Commons in the month of January 1865.

Mississippi
February 1865

*E*van Mac Briber, a black slave, was still looking into the cotton field anticipating someone. His dark eyes glazed while minutes passed by. He took off his brown hat from his head. His clean shaven head was bathed with sweat. He wiped it off with a handkerchief. His newly stitched white suit fitted him well. A cheerful whistling came across the cotton field. In response to that, Evan returned a noise similar to the whistle, but this noise came from the deep of his throat like how a goat herder does. With a smile on his face, he ran along the cotton field. His friends stood on the other side. One short black guy was not dressed properly.

It was a clear indication that he was in a hurry, so he didn't care about his dressing. His name was Antony Cober, who was of the same age as Evan, twenty- three. The other tall black guy called Kim Roo had dressed neatly. He was older than them, nearly thirty.

'We are getting late, Evan. We should be moving quickly.' Antony said to them impatiently. 'We ought to get to Natchez.'

'I don't think we will make,' Kim said in a mild voice.

'Mr President will call at Natchez at two o' clock. Now the time is quarter past one.' Antony said as he looked at his new Zenith watch. He pushed his shirt flap up to his elbow in order for it to be visible to his friends. His face felt proud while he was doing that.

Evan and Kim looked at it surreptitiously. Antony smiled and said; 'No peeping, please.'

'Where did you get it from?' They asked unanimously amused.

'I have got my wages for thirteen years.'

'Lewson gave you money?' Evan enquired.

'Yes, he did. Slavery is illegal now, sir. You understand that, don't you?'

'Yes, I do, but... fucking miser planter.' Evan stopped halfway.

'It is not a precarious thing in this time of context, my friends. We ought to hurry to Natchez to see the president.'

'Yes, that is the important thing we are aiming at,' Antony said.

'What are you waiting for? Come on then.' Evan moved forward. The scorching sun had been casting its merciless heat upon them. Swirling wind flying across the muddy road left behind dust on their way.

'Evan, shall we rent bikes from the shop?'

'Are you crazy, Kim?' Those shops belong to Thadevoos Walter, the white man. Would you dare to dream he would give his bikes to black niggers like us?' Evan responded.

'But slavery has come to an end. It has been outlawed.' Kim responded.

'Since when?' Evan asked in a harsh voice.

'Since 31 January.'

'The law has only been passed by the House of Commons. The president has to sign it, and federal court may review it, so it will take three or four months more to establish as a federal law.'

'In the meantime, we are free, free to think, free to sing a song, free to come outside from the attics of fiefdoms. We are emancipated from the nasty hands of white men,' Antony roared.

On the way, they saw a white boy called Michael Elroy. He was twenty-one, and he was riding a bike towards them. He scanned them eagerly as he was riding it.

'Who is that, Evan?' Kim asked in a soft voice. He pulled over the bike on the way.

'He is the son of Morgan Elroy, the inn-keeper.' Evan replied.

'Yes, I know that son of a bitch Elroy and The Fighting Cock Inn, the inn for the white people only. There was board hanging in the front courtyard saying, "Dogs will be served but not blacks," Antony said.

They were both fearful of each other. 'Don't try to attack him. He might have gangs behind him. If we attempt any unwise assault, we will certainly be in trouble.' Evan said mildly. As they were heading towards him, he reversed his bike and made his way towards where he came from. 'Coward, little monkey.' They laughed.

Natchez was a small town where there weren't many shops. An inn in front of it bore the name The Fighting Cock, opposite to that was a bike shop, another one adjacent to that was possessed by Thadevoos Walter. There was also a restaurant owned by Frodo Jackson. The menu displayed on the blackboard written in white chalk ran like this: 'Today's special: black peas, black monkey's soup, fried black turtle liver, boiled black rice.' All those black stuffs were being served only for the whites. On the corner, there was an old tailoring shop: an old name board bore the name Sisley's Tailoring shop. There were some other small shops selling cigars, beers, and wines. On the right-hand side, the Mississippi river flowed continuously.

When they came along at the town there were around a three hundred enthusiastic people gathered to see President. All of the black people wanted to have a look at the President of United States of America. They were chanting and cheering together. Some of them were applauding and making sounds harmonically. They had been waiting for the president since morning. Although they were in high spirits, they have got new faces and chaste smiles. Elroy came out from the inn. There was a weighty contempt on his face.

'Emancipated black folks,' he cried out.

'Wait, Elroy.' Thadevoos said to him from his shop, 'we will hang those bastards publicly.' Evan overheard the yelling of Thadevoos. He approached him. 'Do you want us hanged?' He said in a threatening tone.

'Hey, hey, listen to me,' he cried out. The mob stopped their celebration and lent their ears to Evan's voice.

'This man wants us to be hanged publicly. Can you hear me?' The crowd clenched their fists in fury and moved towards him. 'Kill that bastard,' someone yelled from the crowd. It was Antony who flew into his shop and pulled off his bikes one by one. After him, Evan got into the shop and threw away all the bike parts out off the shop. Evan was blind with a surge of anger. He pushed a table off to the floor where he found out a matchbox. He lit it and then put it on a pile of old tyres in the corner. Within a minute, the shop was burnt to ashes. Soon, Elroy took off the controversial inn board and made some changes on it, and he was ready to welcome any one regardless of their skin, black, white, yellow or green, he was even ready to welcome a skinless man at that moment. Frodo Jackson's black menu board turned out to be white one.

President turned up at nearly three o' clock in the evening. He sat on black horse cart that came along the Mississippi road. It was his unofficial visit to somewhere to the Mississippi. As the crowd saw him, they roared in a feeling of awe.

'There is Mr Lincoln, our beloved president,' someone roared from the crowd.

'Evan, can you see the president?' Kim asked.

'No, I can't, Kim.'

'Let's push through the crowd, and get ourselves in the front row,' Evan replied.

'That is not as easy as we think, Evan.'

'Let's go to the further end,' Antony yelled.

'That is a bad idea. It will take time,' Evan said.

'Then what we gonna do?' Evan looked around. *It is not easy to get to the front. How can I see the president?* He thought. His eyes got a glimpse of a big sycamore tree close to the road. "That would be a good idea," he said to himself. He ran towards it. Dust swirled across town. There was roaring, applauding, dancing, sound of joy, and shouts of exclamation. Evan climbed up the tree. The thick foliage was an obstruction to see through even though he managed to get to the end of the branch. Now, he could see the President Mr Lincoln. His face lightened up with a smile. President had on a black suit.

Over the suit, there was a coat long enough to cover his knee. His black top hat adorned with a golden lining around it was amazing. He stood up on the open cart and raised his hat and waved towards the crowd. His black long beard was neatly cut and brushed like his hair. There was a smile that spread across his face. When he came under the sycamore tree with a thrust of enthusiasm, or over whelming joy, he turned around quickly to get himself down to see the President closer. While attempting to do that, he dropped his hat, and it came all the way down onto the road in front of president's cart. The driver pulled over the cart, and security aimed their gun up at the tree.

'Who the hell is up there in the tree? Come down or else I will shoot,' one of the security men cried out.

'No... no... no. No need for that.' As Evan came down, he added, 'I am a well-wisher. I won't cause any harm to any other people.'

'Put your hands on your head.' Evan did as they ordered.

'Mr President, I really wanted to see you. The crowd did not let me see you from the ground, so I climbed up in the tree to have a look at you, a historical man.'

Abraham Lincoln dismounted from the cart with a magnanimous smile. He took Evan's brown hat and walked towards him. 'Put down your guns.' he said to the security.

'What is your name please?' Evan's heart pounded as he looked into the president's deep eyes.

I would have annoyed the great man on my thoughtless deed. What's his eyes saying to me? His smile is attractive but no hint of anything, enigmatic gestures.

'Evan Mac Briber, sir.' His eyes were filled with tears in a sudden thrust of happiness. *'I am at your feet president.'*

Mr Lincoln placed his hat on his head.

'I am not a historian. I am a human like you. Even though our skin is different, our blood colour is alike. That makes our race unique. I have done my duty, that's it. If that makes you people proud, I am happy.' He turned around and settled again on the cart that moved swiftly along the Mississippi road. The crowd cheered again.

Eva De Casa, a young white girl, was sitting on the porch of her home. She seemed to be engrossed with knitting her green muffler from a knit yarn using two black needles simultaneously. She looked like an expert at it. She had a flat cotton cap on her head. White hair slipped down from inside the cap, and it covered her smooth face, which almost covered her deep blue eyes. Her dark and long eye lashes did not even blink for a minute. She had a long pink skirt and a white cardigan. Her gestures and movements of her face and body were quite fit and natural for a twenty-year-old girl. She didn't seem to be impatient as she heard the ascending footsteps of Evan. She withdrew her eyes and looked at him. Again, she started knitting.

'Did you see the president?' she asked, as she continued.

'I did,' he responded. 'Not only that. I was blessed with his blessings. He spoke to me.'

'Did he?' Eva raised her eyes. Then, she stayed silent for a moment. Evan turned around.

'What is your future plan? Will you live here?'

'Not yet decided.'

'You are free now. You can go anywhere in America.'

'Yes, first, I need to find a job.'

'Are you not going anywhere?' Planter Sebastian Sholto appeared. His voice trembled with anger. His black thick trucker-style moustache covered his lower lip. As he parted both sides with his black flat comb, he flashed his white teeth.

'You can't go anywhere from here, you nigger,' he roared.

'Yes, I can go wherever I want. I am free now.'

'America is only for white people like us. Whatever the law is I don't care. That foolish president doesn't care about people like us, planters, and investors. Where will we get labourers from?'

'That's the only problem that lay before you.'

'How dare you speak to me like that? Who gave you the right to speak to me in an authoritative manner?' He went behind the back of the house and fetched one long bull whip.

'This is enough for you to be brought under my control.'

'Papa.' Eva came forward and tried to stop him.

'Get out of my way, you little whore.' He pushed her away. She fell down on the ground. As Sholto waved the whip at him, for the first time in Evan's life, he took action to stop Sholto doing the diabolic deed. Evan jumped up using his right leg to get close to him, and within a fraction of second he punched Sholto's face; Sholto was on the ground.

'The whip was smeared with my blood numerous times. I won't let you do it again.' Evan was out of breath in a surge of anger. Evan turned around and went back. Eva looked at him until he disappeared.

Antony Cober was in a bit of a hurry to make vegetable soup. He poured hot soup into a small bowl and also prepared butter peas.

'Evan, you did a foolish thing. Do you know that?' Antony was a bit anxious.

'I do, Antony, but how would it be possible to suffer this torturing on and on?' He settled on a wooden chair.

'Look, you had to handle the situation wisely. I mean wisely. Are you with me?'

'We are not slaves any more, Antony.' His voice trembled. 'We aren't born to be slaves.' They kept quiet for a moment; they looked each other, and sighed sadly.

'That is the federal rule of America after the review. As you said, it may take time to come into action. I don't know what the white men will do, Evan. They might kill you in the first place.' He paced up and down.

After some heavy thuds of footsteps, the door flew open and Charles Lewson entered. The door closed behind him. His golden-framed spectacles slipped to the tip of his nose. He had a clean shaven face and, deep hawk eyes.

'Mr Charles.' Antony bowed his head towards him.

'No, no, Antony, there is no need for that. I have told you, haven't I?'

'You deserve respect and attention, Mr Charles.' Antony shrugged.

'You got company.' He peeped at Evan over Antony's shoulder. 'What is your name?' He held Evan's icy hand.

'Evan.' He stood up and shook his hand. He tried to smile, but it came out as a smirk.

'You are shivering, Evan. There is no cold out there. Warm enough. Then what makes you shiver?'

'His situation, Mr Charles,' Antony said mildly.

'What situation are you in, Evan?' He pushed up his spectacles with his fore finger and enquired.

Evan narrated the event carefully and ended up in tears.

'Oh, you are in a bad situation. I overheard from Thadevoos about the incident. I am pretty sure, Evan that they are hunting for you. Either you have to flee Mississippi or find a safe hideout. If they find you, they will peel off your skin for sure.'

There was a clattering sound coming from the front gate, followed by the sound of horse hooves. Charles slowly drew back the curtain.

'I was right, Evan. They are here for you, and they started their job.'

'Please don't let them see me.' His heartbeats echoed in his ears; his forehead bathed with sweat. Charles scanned his eyes.

'Antony, take him to the attic of the house. We have a big barn. He can hide in.'

As they moved from there, someone knocked the door. Charles opened the door. There stood Sebastian Sholto with a gun on his shoulder. There three men on the horses, Thadevoos Walter, Frodo Jackson, and Morgan Elroy, had guns on the shoulders; their faces were serious and red in show of anger. Michael Elroy was on the bike. He had a dagger in his hand.

'Yes Mr Sholto, how may I help you, and what can I offer you and your beloved men?' Charles said in a sarcastic voice.

'I am not here for fun, Charles. I want a bloody nigger.'

'I am not keeping any nigger here.'

'We want to make it sure.' Thadevoos roared.

'People in the Mississippi know about you that you are a nigger lover,' Jackson cried out.

'I never pointed a gun at them. I have never used a whip on their naked body. I consider them as humans. Neither of you did that.'

'Nigger is always a nigger. Slaves are always slaves. Tell me where Evan is? We have information that he will be here. His friend Antony is here, so he may have come here.'

'May have come here, but he is not here, Sholto.'

'Get out of my way, Charles.' Sholto cried as he forcibly broke into the house. Charles quickly fetched his gun from the wall and pointed it at Sholto, before he could move inside the house.

'I can hear your perceived heartbeats underneath my gun barrel. If you dare to move further.' Charles yelled. His spectacles slipped to the tip of his nose. Sholto looked into his eyes. He sensed the weighty vexation in his eyes. 'My gun is loaded. I have never used it. Don't make me use it. I told you I am not protecting anyone here. Go, Sholto, go'

'You know what he did to me.'

'As you sow, so shall you reap.'

'I will kill him.' Sholto cried out. 'That will be a lesson for all the niggers and nigger lovers, I will burn him alive.' Horses whined, and the sound of their horses' hooves slowly died out with the breeze.

'Antony,' Charles called him mildly and handover him the gun and said. 'Load the gun as fast as you can.'

'It has been eight days since I came here.' Evan said to Antony while he ate a sandwich.

'You are not free now, Evan,' Antony returned. 'They have all been running amok for you for the last eight days.'

'I just want to convince one person that I am still alive.'

'Who the hell on earth is that, Evan?'

'None other than Eva.'

'Sholto's daughter?'

'Not really, his step-daughter actually.'

'What is the relationship between the both of you?'

'She is as same as me, Antony. She is a slave under the roof. She is in an ultimate prison. Sholto is a devil. He never took care of her.'

'That is not a matter for us, Evan.'

'Yes, it is.' His voice trembled. 'Kindly do me a favour, Antony. I'll write a letter to her that I am still alive. I want to let her know. Could you please hand it out to her?' His eyes flashed in a token of expectation.

'Write a letter?' Antony laughed. 'How would you write a letter? Do you know how to write? You are an illiterate little devil.'

'Yes, I know. Eva taught me how to write and read.'

'Good God, you know learning is an offence amongst the black slaves, don't you?'

'I do, but understanding the world is not an offence, Antony. Will you do me a favour?'

After a long silence, Antony replied, 'I will.' He walked up to the door and turned around. His face was serious thinking something seriously. 'By the way, Evan did you read any books? I mean fiction.' Evan was surprised. 'Why are you asking me such a stupid question?'

'No, it is not a stupid question.'

'Of course, I read some world classics written by Dickens, Dumas.'

'You are lucky, Evan. I wish I could, but I don't know how to read. Mr Charles got some books. Sometimes I open the book and look at the letters with blank eyes, but I have never read a single line. You are lucky.' His words were broken, and he left by putting the hat back on his head.

As Antony moved across the cotton field, he barely had any hope that he could fulfil the promise. Kim was just behind him. The time was nearly midnight.

'Are you sure?' Kim stopped and asked.

'What am I sure about?'

'That you are able to deliver the letter?'

'I am not sure, but we will try.' As they headed forward, they could see Sholto's house. All the windows were dark except the one in the corner; a feeble light came from the narrow window.

'Time is nearly midnight. She might be asleep for sure.' Kim said in a trembling voice. Without giving any answer, Antony advanced.

Eva De Casa was sweating all over; she was tired and in low spirit. Her white hair was smeared with sweat. She was really in a hurry to finish filling up the barn with grain. Time had been ticking away. Ascending foot steps made her hurry a bit more. Sholto stood revealed in front of her.

'Look, you nasty bitch,' he roared. He held an open can of beer. He gulped down the beer and wiped his thick lips with the sleeve of his dark-coloured shirt. 'I've told you about the timing of a work. You would have to finish this work before midnight, but you've made it late.' He advanced towards her and poured the cold beer on her head.

'Come on, make it fast. There are two more barns out there in the corner. Look. Fill that up, or you are not going to sleep tonight.' He retired with a victorious smile on his face.

Eva knelt down, placed her face in her palms, and cried like a child. As Antony and Kim got close to the window, they could see a dark figure kneeling down on the floor. Antony knocked on the window hesitantly.

'Eva, open the window. It's me Antony.' He said in a low voice as he was tapping on the window. Suddenly, the window flew open, making a high-pitched creaking sound.

'Who, *who* is that?' She enquired in a hoarse whisper.

'Antony, it's Antony and Kim. We are friends with Evan, the black slave.'

'Happy to meet you, Eva,' Kim said. 'It's the first time I've seen you. As Evan said, you are beautiful. Yes, indeed!, I can even tell that in this darkness, although I'm unhappy to see you for the first time in the middle of the night in situation like this.' Kim sighed.

Eva tried to smile, but she could not force herself. Instead, her eyes were filled up with tears. 'I am truly pleased to see you both.' There was cold beer still dripping down from her hair.

'You smell of beer. Have you been drinking?' Antony enquired.

'No, he poured beer on my head,' she cried hopelessly. 'Save me from this hell. Save me.'

Kim and Antony stood motionless. Cold wind hit their faces, and the window creaked. They felt pain in their hearts. Their hearts wished to disclose the joy of liberation, one moment of entire emancipation, to live like human beings, to be free from the clutches of the damned black chain, the chain of slavery. Antony pressed down on her cold hand to console her.

'We are helpless, Eva.' His voice was filled with rage. 'But one day, you'll be free. We are the messengers. We were told to hand you a letter from Evan.'

'Where is he?' she asked in a high tone.

'I hope every detail will be in the letter. Here it is.'

Antony handed the letter to her.

'Who's there?' a voice called out. Following that, there was the sound of footsteps. Sholto appeared in the room, and he sped towards the window. He was carrying a gun on his shoulder. He still had a can of beer in his hand. The window was closed. He opened the window and scanned outside. All he saw was cotton fields blanketed with thick darkness. There was no movement or anything suspicious.

'Who were you speaking to?' He turned around and looked at her surreptitiously.

She was trembling. 'I am speaking only to you now. You hear me, don't you?'

He splashed more cold beer on her face and threw the empty can into the corner.

'I haven't spoken to anyone else.'

As he surveyed her top to bottom, he saw something between her white top and wet body. It looked like the tip of a white paper. He moved quickly and fetched the letter.

She stood frozen.

He read it out. 'Eva, I am alive. I will find a way to get you out from that hell at once. More details will be sent soon. As soon as you got the letter, destroy it.'

Sholto nearly broke into laugh, but he suppressed it.

'Oh, I'm sorry, Eva. Sorry for the interference.' Sholto gave the letter back to her and walked away.

Eva sighed in token of disbelief.

'Keep doing your job, you bitch. I haven't got time to worry about such trivial things.'

Eva pressed the letter to her lips and smiled.

As soon as Antony and Kim arrived at Charles' house, they gulped a jug of water. They wiped their sweaty faces with their sleeves and sat down. Still they were gasping.

'Did you make it?' Evan asked from the attic. His voice trembled with anxiety.

'What Goddamn thing did you write in the letter?' Kim was shivering.

'You had better leave here soon,' Antony whispered. 'May I ask you a private question? Sorry to ask you; but what was the content of the letter?'

'Sholto must have seen that letter we made a narrow escape. Tell us Evan'. Kim demanded.

'Nothing to worry about. I haven't done anything wrong. There is no mention in the letter about anything in which they can trace back to me,' Evan responded. That piece of information must have pacified them. They sat still for a long time.

'I don't know how we could get rid of these white folks. We have got freedom the sweetest of all, yet it still feels bitter.' Evan came down to the room.

'Poor, Eva. She is still a labouring slave, under his rugged command.' Kim muttered.

'We should save her from that hell.' Evan told them, but he sounded unsure.

'As you said, are you sure that the letter was written by Evan the nigger?' Morgan Elroy puffed on a cigar. His black cowboy hat covered his face.

'I am pretty sure of it. The letter was written by that nigger.' Sholto settled himself on a stool and looked at Morgan. 'I was surprised when I saw the letter, but somehow I suppressed my amusements. I knew that the man we are looking for might have written it.'

'That is quite funny,' Sisley said as she gulped down a beer. 'How could it be possible for a nigger who doesn't know to write or read?'

'Yes that is right.' Frodo Jackson nodded. 'It is impossible for the blacks to write and read English.'

'Believe me; the letter looked like just a scribble.' Sholto looked around and roared with laughter.

'This is very entertaining, a black man who knows how to write letters sent it to a girl and. ...' Morgan nodded and threw the cigar into his boot tip. 'Where is the letter Sholto? May we see it?'

'I gave it back to Eva. If she becomes suspicious of me, then we won't get any news about him. I need him alive.' His face darkened.

'Who might have taught him how to write then?' Sisley narrowed her eyes. 'Does Eva know how to read and write?'

'Yes, she does.' Sholto responded.

'Ha.... ha. Then everything is clear.' Frodo Jackson said. 'She did a culpable crime. That nasty one did teach him English. She deserves to die.' Frodo Jackson turned around and fetched his gun from the table. 'She must die.'

'Don't be in a hurry, Frodo,' Morgan said. 'If he is here in Natchez, he will certainly be in Charles's house, who is the only white man protecting the coloured ones. So we should keep watching his house day and night. We can surely trust Michael my son and his gangs. Eva's crime should also be punished. She must pay for what she's done.'

Frodo Jackson's restaurant was a secret place for them to execute their diabolic plan. Michael Elroy and his gangs were appointed to watch Charles's house to catch any trace of Evan. They placed themselves camouflaged in the middle of the cotton fields, day and night.

Two days later, Kim Roo and Antony Cober were close to Sholto's house on a moonlit midnight. They were moving across the cotton fields.

'How could we see Eva?' Kim enquired.

'We will try to meet her. We need to deliver the letter.'

'But how?'

'Trust me, there'll be a way.'

Some thirty feet behind them, Michael Elroy and his gangs had an eye on them.

'Keep the distance with them always,' Michael said. The others nodded. 'Okay, I'm moving towards the main road so I can get my bike. I need to get at Sholto's house and let him know that niggers are heading towards him, okay?'

'Okay, you go and let him know. We will follow them.' Justin one of the gang members said.

'Don't let them out of your sight.'

'No, we won't.'

Michael headed to main road.

'All right, look the same window around the corner. There comes candlelight through the glass. Let's move.' Antony said to Kim as they approached Sholto's house.

Eva was sitting in the same place where she had been the last time.

Kim knocked on the window.

Eva raised her face, which was bathed with sweat; her face looked lifeless. She came close to the window and opened it.

'Eva, here is another letter from Evan. Are you all right?' Kim narrowed his eyes.

'Yes... yes.' she replied absently.

'Okay, may be you should write a letter in response to this letter. We don't have much time to speak. We'll be back around the same time tomorrow night. Be prepared. You're going to be free from this hell soon enough.'

Eva smiled wryly.

Soon they disappeared from there into the moonlit night.

There was laughter from the corner of the room. Sholto lit another candle, his cruel face slowly perceptible as the candle came alive. He lowered his gun, which he had been pointing towards her.

'Good girl.' He got to his feet.

Michael Elroy appeared from the darkness behind him, and his rowdy accomplices moved towards her. They had been hiding themselves in the darkness.

'Your effort was truly appreciated, young Elroy. You let me know everything in a timely manner.'

Michael broadened his shoulders in a show of pride.

As they came closer to Eva, she screwed the letter into a ball and put it in her mouth.

'You bitch, how dare you? Spit it out. Come on, spit it out!' Sholto strangled her. Michael held tightly on to her hair and made her kneel down.

Sholto pressed his finger on her cheek as the pain developed. Eventually, she opened her mouth. He put his fingers in and retrieved the wet letter from her mouth.

Sholto slapped her face. It caused blood to erupt and run down from her nose.

'I won't cheat him.' She sobbed inconsolably.

'You are a nigger lover.'

Michael pushed her down.

Sholto held the letter flat on the table. Even though the letters on it were illegible, he made it out slowly and carefully.

'Eva, you'll no longer be under Sholto's feet. I am planning something which would help us to escape this nasty place among these rowdy white folks. The sameness of our life situation has to be changed forever. I know how much you are suffering from Sholto, the rascal. The callous epoch of our life will come to an end. We are in same boat. Tomorrow night, Antony and Kim will come. Please write in respond to this. In three days, we will get out from here. America is wide enough.'

Sholto looked at Eva who was sitting on the floor like a child. Her nose was still bleeding.

'You are hoping against hope, Eva,' Sholto cried. 'You won't go anywhere and neither will he.'

Early the next morning, Morgan, Frodo Jackson, Walter, Sisley, and all the other whites gathered in Sholto's house.

'Well, do we have any idea where the nigger is?' Frodo Jackson asked Sholto. He removed his hat.

'He is in Charles Lewson's house'. Michel piped up.

'Then let's go and get him.' Morgan said.

'Don't be a fool.' Sisley raised her voice, as she bounced up and down and lit a cigar.

'It is not the wisest decision to get him from there. Not only Charles but some other white people are also nigger lovers.' Sisley stopped short and continued quickly.

'Wait, I have an idea. Why do we have to labour to get him out of the house?' She smiled and looked at Eva. 'Would he distrust Eva?'A horrid smile appeared on her face. All of them kept quiet. 'He really loves her. Oh god, a nigger loves her!' She sighed.

'Anyway she should write him a letter.'

After a while, all of them laughed.

'Ha... ha... easy to get him out,' Sholto yelled. 'Get a pen and paper, Michael.'

'Bring her here, close to the table,' Frodo Jackson said.

Michael and Justin dragged her to the table. The blood on her nose had dried, but tears were trickling down her cheeks.

'I won't do that,' she whispered. She was placed on a wooden stool, and was provided with pen and paper.

'What's the difference between me and you?' Sisley settled herself in the chair opposite her. 'Put down what I'm saying, Eva.' Her eyes stuck on Eva's face. 'Do what I say.'

'I won't do it. I can't.' Her voice came out between sobs.

'Do what she is saying.' Sholto put the gun to her head. 'As you know, I won't hesitate to pull the trigger.'

With a quivering hand, Eva managed to fetch the pen.

Sisley continued, 'So what's his name?' She asked Sholto.

'Evan,' he replied.

'Evan, the situation is obviously mounting pressure on me.' With a devilish smile, Sisley started.

Eva's hand shivered. Slowly, she started writing.

'Sholto, the uncouth man, might pulverise me at any time. My hands and legs are tightened with chains. I can't get free from here. My death will be under Sholto's feet. He thinks I'm an animal. Day and night, I have been working. Sometimes I don't get food. Please save me from this hell as soon as possible. I can no longer suffer this slavery. Evan, make a plan and let me know. I can come with you any time. If my mother was alive, I wouldn't have to suffer all these miseries. Please lent me your hand at this moment of crisis. I trust you, Evan. Please write to me as soon as possible.'

Evan lowered the candle from the table to the floor.

Antony and Kim looked at him anxiously.

After reading the letter, he closed his eyes, thinking.

'What do you want to do Evan?' Antony asked him.

'We have to flee from there,' Evan said. 'How long do I have to hide myself in this attic?'

'But how?'Antony asked. 'How would you escape from here? The white folks must have their eyes on us. Deceiving them will not be easy.'

'I'll write a letter to her in which I'll explain my plan to escape from here.' He started to make up his mind to escape from here to somewhere else in America. 'Evan.' Antony grabbed his hand. 'We would be happy if you could manage to escape from here, but it's really unsafe.'

'We really need to make a proper plan, or else, it won't work.' Kim said.

'As soon as she gets away from Sholto's house, we must be ready to get out of town.' Antony said. 'We need transportation.'

'Going by road would put us in peril,' Evan stated. 'The best way is by river.'

'By river!' they exclaimed. 'But how?'

'Kim, your master Jim Paxton possesses a fishing boat, doesn't he?'

'Yes, he does'. Kim answered.

'Kim, tonight you need to procure that boat. I know it's really hard to come by, indeed. However, could you please help me?' Evan pressed Kim's ice cold hand towards his beating heart. Kim realised his fiery expectation. 'Will you Kim?' His voice trembled. Kim tapped on his shoulder and nodded.

'Today's a bad day for me, a filthy bad day. Oh, I'm really exhausted.' Jim Paxton came back to his house. As he scurried up to it, he was dodging as if he were drunk. He untied his heavy boots.

'Master.' Kim appeared.

'It is good to see you. Where have you been? Are you all right? I thought you had run away from here.'

'I would have gone, but I didn't want to leave you alone.'

'You think you are doing a favour to me, Kim,' he said in a mild voice, and he scanned Kim's face. Kim saw kindness and affection in his deep eyes. His master was a paradigm of how good masters should be. Whenever he saw his master, he felt respect and affection. Jim Paxton moved back to the house carrying a candle. He was holding a fishing hook. He needed it to be placed safely in an iron box. He opened the box and made sure all his stuffs are correct in position and exact in numbers by counting it. Kim was accustomed to see his routine duty every night since he came in his house.

'So you think you are doing a favour to me?'

Jim placed the candle to see Kim's face. Kim looked into his eyes and said,

'Yes, I am, because I like you. You consider me to be a human. I am a coloured man, a slave, but... but I feel pain. I have dreams, and emotions. However you are the most agreeable man I have ever met.'

'You could have gone. I didn't stop you?' He paused. 'Did I?'

'No one stopped me. 'Kim looked into the darkness, 'But you were alone master.' They kept quiet for a moment.

'Why didn't I go somewhere in America? I could have, but what did stop me to walk away from this little man's shadow.' Kim raised his eyes and searched his master's feelings and thoughts in the bottom of his heart. Jim twisted his face away from him; he must have known that Kim sought for his sentiments as he used to be. He lowered the candle and walked back to

the house. Kim stood alone in the dark. He never asked the question by himself. '*I was enjoying the sweetness of so- called unseeable slavery in the shadow of my master, the little man.*' Kim nodded with a sigh.

'Thanks for not letting me down, Kim,' He said in his mild voice. Kim got back in the room where Jim had a glass of wine. Jim imbibed a little and then continued,

'Look, I am an old man. My wife is no more, but you have helped me all these years to get things done. Now you are free. We are equal in America, and you can go wherever you want.' After a pause, he continued, 'I am really hungry Kim.'

'Soup is on the table, master.'

'Today, I didn't have anything.' Whilst he was gulping down the vegetable soup, he muttered, 'You know, today, I didn't have any luck. I couldn't catch any fish.'

'Master, let me ask one question. It is a humble request rather than a question. Could I borrow your fishing boat?' After a moment, Jim Paxton laughed and responded.

'Kim, fishing is not a child's play.'

'Master.' Kim interrupted, 'this isn't for fishing.'

Jim put his half emptied soup bowl down upon the table carefully and looked at him.

'What do you mean?' He narrowed his eyes.

Kim explained everything. Jim listened carefully.

'I could have stolen your boat, but I didn't want to do that. I want to be honest as you taught me.'

Jim Paxton lit a cigar. 'This is really a dangerous game. I know those white rascals very well, and however, I will help your friends. I will come by myself, tomorrow by midnight. I would be there on my boat down to Mississippi river. Once they get in my boat, I will oar downstream and will let them go where I feel it is a safe haven.' As he was saying it, his eyes scintillated in a thrust of overwhelm.

'*My master, your benevolence, your hospitable heart, your pure sentiments will always be indefatigable in my heart forever.*'

'So tomorrow night will be the most dangerous and appalling.' Evan said to Kim and Antony. They sat on chairs around a table where a candle was placed on the middle of the table.

'What time do you prefer, Evan?' Kim asked. 'My master will be on the river by midnight.'

'Okay, that is fine.' Evan narrowed his eyes. 'I think morning two o' clock would be the better time.'

'Then you will have to write a letter to Eva. We will hand it tonight,' Antony said.

'No, I am not going to write any letter tonight. I don't feel to write. Instead, you have to speak to her and let her know the time.'

'It is not possible to speak to her during midnight,' Antony interrupted.

'Three words only.' Evan kept quiet. 'Be ready at two o' clock.'

Michael and his gangs were up to date with their duty. As they were sincerely dutiful, they prepared a letter for Evan before nightfall. In which she had been forced to write him to turn up by midnight. As the clock was ticking away, the same window was lit with candlelight. Eva was placed in the chair. From the darkness she knew three guns were pointing towards her body.

'No interaction. Just hand the letter.' Sholto's harsh voice came from darkness. She prayed. She looked into the darkness and the window at the same time. There was a slow movement of shadows from other side of the window. Then, it developed into a bigger one. Later, it came closer to the window and then halted for a second. Now she heard the knock on the window. Window flew open. Without saying a word, she ejected her hand and handed the letter to Antony. The window slammed close.

'It says midnight tomorrow.' Evan read it and looked at them.

'We could not say a word,' Antony said.

'May be this would be the convenient time for her,' Kim said.

Evan pressed the letter to his lips. *Smell of lavender. That's her smell.* He smiled as he saw Eva in front of his naked eyes.

The next night, Jim Paxton was getting ready to go for the anticipated rescue mission. The time was nearly ten. As Jim went close to his boat, Morgan and Michael Elroy appeared ahead from the darkness.

'Hi, Jim,' they came close to him. 'Whatever you were thinking of doing won't work.'

'Hey boys, move out off my way.' Jim stepped up.

'You are a nigger lover. You're doing a favour for the coloured.'

Jim was a bit surprised; however, he tried to conceal it. *'How would these guys know about it? Situation is very dangerous than I think. Did I under estimate these guys? Damn shit. I am a fool.'* Within a fraction of a second, some one crouched in the boat poured kerosene on it.

'Don't do it, boys.' Jim tried to run to the boat, but before he could, he was grounded by a huge blow to his face. His boat burnt to ashes with in a few minutes, and he was dragged into his house.

'We're gonna peel off that bloody nigger lover's skin,' someone yelled.

As Evan moved along the cotton field, his mind was clinging to sweet memories. The unleashed reminiscence pushed him off from time to time. His face was serious and hard like an unflagging warrior. He wore a newly stitched suit which Antony and Kim presented him.

As he approached Sholto's house, the raging curiosity weakened his nerves. He could hear his heartbeats. They echoed in his ears. There was no light. Evan moved across the pavement into the side room. *'Liberation is starting from where I was a slave.'* There was no sign of anyone.

Suddenly, the front door flew open. Following that, he heard Eva's broken voice. 'Get away, Evan. Get away!'

The voice ended, and the door slammed.

Evan stood still for a moment. Numbness swept all over his body. He sensed the danger, and scurried to the road and ran as quickly as possible.

Halfway down, he met Antony who was on a bike.

'Evan, we were cheated. She cheated us. Jim was attacked by the gangs and he is under their custody.'

Evan stood motionless.

'Get on the bike! We have to get away from here without wasting any more time.' Evan jumped on the bike. Behind them, the sound of horses' hooves echoed followed by a gunshot. The bullet pierced Antony's chest, and he fell over. Blood gushed out.

'Evan, get away from here. Escape, and don't let them catch you,' he insisted.

'Don't bother about me, my friend.'

As Evan was heading away, he heard Antony's last word, 'Give me a drop of water.'

Again he heard two gunshots.

'Hey, nigger, it's good for you to stop there, or else I will shoot you,' Sebastian Sholto's harsh and piercing voice interrupted.

Evan ran into the cotton field, with his heart pounding. He ran wildly, gasping and cursing himself, his eyes filling with tears. The cotton field seemed endless.

At the end of the field, some rowdy boys were eagerly waiting for Evan; having known Evan would come and fall into their murderous clutches. Evan stood revealed in front of them. Like wild animals, they pounced on him and tied up his hands.

'Do you think us fools, you dirty bastard?' Michael Elroy pounded on him and smashed him on the face. 'Tie him up properly and drag him. Don't let him walk.' Justin tied the rope on to his bike, and they dragged him along the road until they reached the sycamore tree. Under the sycamore tree, wooden benches and stools were arranged. They had been emblazoned with red velvet cloths with frills on them. Lights from the Kerosene lamps surrounded the sycamore tree.

'We erected it.' Morgan Elroy sat on a platform around the sycamore tree, and he said proudly. As he said it, his eyes stared at Evan piercingly. 'It took three days to finish, specially designed for a nigger.'

There was a spontaneous laughter from the gang.

Right on top of the platform were two ropes with a loop in them, ready to hang people. Evan looked at it and realised that the hours had been counted for him. His eyes filled up, but he did not feel the fear at all. His body was aching. His new garments were torn apart, and blood stains were on them. Since he did not fear he stood on his feet and asked,

'Hey bloody white men, I'm really confused about those loops in the ropes. There's one for me, but would you please be kind enough to tell me who the second loop is for?'

'Look at him,' Elroy responded. 'He has suffered a lot of torments by now, but still he has the guts to speak out and mock us,' he stood on his feet.

'Answer my question, you bloody white men!'

'How dare you speak me like that?' Elroy advanced and hit him on the face.

'You're barbarian! My tooth!' Evan spat it to the ground with blood. 'Look, I've lost tooth. It's not a good idea to tie my hands and hit me like this. If you are real white man who has courage and courtesy, you must untie me and fight with me. Do you dare do it?'

Elroy seemed a bit nervous and didn't respond.

Evan laughed disparagingly.

'You'll regret it, nigger,' Elroy responded finally, 'Do you want to know who the second person is who we're going to hang?'

Horse hooves echoed out behind them, and with a proud face like an adjudicator, Sebastian Sholto appeared with his gun. He dismounted the horse.

'So those two black niggers were shot dead,' he said in a proud voice. 'America is the land for white people like us.'

'You want coloured ones, and their muscle power to plough the land, to sow the seeds, and to harvest the crops.' Evan raised his voice, 'You want black young ladies for your sexual needs, regardless of their age. You raped a small girl in a solitary farm away from Mississippi two years ago. Do you remember what you told us and, what your excuses were? When it's dark, all ladies are same. All ladies have the same vagina.'

'Yes, I did. I don't disagree with that,' Sholto responded with a laugh.

Soon Sisley and Thadevoos Walter appeared there on horses. Eva was lying across the horse which was being ridden by Frodo Jackson. He threw her on to the ground, like a sack of ragged clothes. She landed helplessly on the dusty ground.

'Do you want to know, who the second loop is for?' Elroy cried, 'For your beautiful loved one, the bitch.' Elroy's face raged, and materialised a victorious smile.

Evan was shocked on his comments.

'Eva.'

He knelt down on the ground and sobbed. His undaunted heart throbbed. He raised his eyes and looked at the beautiful face.

'This whore cheated you,' Sholto cried out. 'This fate came upon you because of her.'

Her beautiful face was swollen. The dishevelled woman lifted her saddened eyes towards Evan, they had no hope in them. There was no love and affection in them. Only consternation was visible in her deep blue eyes. She couldn't speak to him as her mouth was filled with tattered clothes, leaving her breath heavily. She got to her feet. She clutched on to the trunk of the sycamore tree.

When she noticed the rope and the loops, she became horribly frightened and ran towards Evan, but before she could reach him, a heavy blow from Frodo Jackson knocked her down to the ground.

'You are a traitor,' Evan said in a soft voice. 'I know that all you whites have the same temperaments, but I forgot that *you* have the same skin as them. But I wouldn't have dreamt that you would send me to death. You called me to your house and deceived me.' Evan got to his feet and spat on her face.

Eva looked at him with empty eyes. She could only cry.

Sisley placed different kinds of beer, wines, and whisky on the benches. The white people sat wherever there was a space available.

'What about the other two niggers?' Sisley lit a cigar and asked Morgan Elroy.

'Since they hadn't done too much to us, we didn't want them to be hanged.' He looked at Sholto. 'Instead, we shot them dead. One nigger was hiding in Jim Paxton's house. As soon as we saw him, I killed him and mutilated his body and threw it in the Mississippi river. The other one we cut his body in to pieces and burnt the remains to ashes in fireplace. We were lucky enough to have healthy accomplices with us to execute that in time.'

'You bastards.' Thadevoos Walter raised his hat in a token of respect.

'This one is the troublemaker.' Sholto nodded at Evan. 'Did you think the president, sadly he was assassinated,' a smirk appeared on Sholto's face, 'gave you an opportunity to equalise both white and black? No, you coloured people's bad fate is starting from now onwards. Your people will be hanged publicly. This will be the commencing event.' He drank whisky. Michael Elroy and his gang were intoxicated, and he came forward.

'As we are young, we have a request. We have got a young and beautiful damsel here. Before sending her to be hanged, we need to have some fun.'

'What are you up to?' Sisley asked.

'It would be very fun to see a lady hanged naked. Wouldn't that be fun, boys?' They raised their beers approvingly.

'Look, they're mesmerized by the beauty of this damsel.'

'We wouldn't have any problem with that.' Sisley chuckled.

'Let me clarify what she has done and the culpable crimes which she has committed,' Thadevoos Walter said with the authenticity of a judge. 'Crime number one is that she taught him English, which we can't forgive at all. It shouldn't have happened since acquiring knowledge and education are the rights for white people only. The second crime is that she has fallen in love with a nigger, which was highly unlikely to have happened. It is reckless and shameful for the whites. The third crime is that she planned to elope with this bloody nigger. As he had already been giving us so much trouble, we have made a decision that only death will be the penalty for them in order to satisfy us.'

All the whites seemed to be pleased with the adjudication of Thadevoos.

'Take off her dress,' Michael Elroy cried out. His gang jumped up and with in a fraction of second they had torn her clothes into pieces.

'Look at her. Fucking hell!' Michael Elroy cried out frantically.

Her white body was shivering. She tried to conceal her bosoms with her bruised cuffed arms, but Elroy brought them apart in order for them to be visible to all the good men.

'It drives me crazy, you fuckers.' Elroy ejaculated.

There was a helpless groan from Eva, her watery eyes still crying endlessly.

'That embarrassment is enough!' Evan cried out. 'If you want to hang us, then do it.'

Above them the leaves of the sycamore tree slowly danced as the gentle breeze brushed them. *The same sycamore tree on which Evan mounted to see the great President Abraham Lincoln.* Evan sighed. The cloudy sky did not let the moon shine out. It was still very dark and gloomy.

Elroy and his gang dragged Eva to the river bank and raped. The only voice of protest was Evan's. When they brought her back, she looked like a skinless creature. Her thighs were wet with urine, and her eyes, lips, and bosoms everywhere was bruised and bleeding.

'Hang him. I want to see him die,' Sholto cried out.

The Elroys came up and fixed the loop on his neck.

'Ha... there was a nigger here.' Walter raised his beer. 'He had an ambition to elope with a white chaste foolish lady, whom he had trusted a lot, and since he has trusted her like his own blood, she was perspicaciously setting a trap by inviting him to go with her to somewhere in America to lead a peaceful life. As he knew the letters which has been taught by the poor chaste girl, he could not have perceived the danger in the letters. He came along and fell in the clutches of murderers. Thus our damsel trapped her loved one.'

'Okay, that was a good narration, wasn't it?' Sisley said. 'Hang him,' she said with an authenticity of an executioner.

Before Evan was hoisted into the air, he looked at Eva. His eyes were filled with tears, and he said to her,

'You too Eva.'

Eva closed her eyes. She didn't understand what he meant by that. 'Did he think that I'm also part of this diabolic plan to trap him, or was that a pity word from the bottom of his heart that I'm dying with him too?' Eva asked to herself. She could not pacify her sorrow. Something had dropped inside her.

'Oh, Evan, let me tell you with an unfathomable purity of my heart and with an unflagging and relentless excellence of thoughts and feelings that I really love you.' Her heartbeat heavily, and her eyes were watery. The next second, she was taken into the air, her neck tightened. She could see Evan hanged close to her. His life had been swept away from his body minutes ago.

Before her eyes were covered with darkness, she could hear the laughter from the ground. As she approached her final gasps, she told herself;

'Yes, me too, Evan.'

The Dilemma of Gandhi

I am not what I used to be since I haven't got a spirit on my body.

A body with out a spirit precisely is a life less one as same as myself.

I have been fixed up here for more than sixty years just like a rock under the scorching heat of sun and in ice cold wind.

None opened umbrella over my head while raining. When sun was penetrating its heat up on my body, there had been no place to hide myself and there would never be.

I am Mohandas Karamchand Gandhi. I was the driving force to establish a new country, and my people consider me as the father of their nation as an honorific title.

I preached my people Ahimsa, which means non-violence, and I fought against untouchability, and led India to independence along with the brave hearts of youth during that time.

We shed blood. We sacrificed our lives to gain liberation from British raj.

Now what is the fate of me?

I haven't got independence since India has got that sweetest and utmost unimaginable truth 'Independence.'

I am a five-feet-three-inch-tall-stone-made black sculpture standing in the middle of Gandhi Park having a walking stick in my hand. I am carved exactly how Churchill called me, 'Half naked Fakir.'

My people did it to me and they excel themselves at moulding me as same as I was in fresh flesh and blood.

They have tied me up using a chain. My whole body is aching. My feet are swollen. How is it possible to stand up since 1950? They have behaved to me ruthlessly. There is no point of me being exasperated. Who cares about that?

I don't know how many freedom fighters had been fixed up like me. There could be some of them who have same fate as me.

I am so helpless for they might endure agony. They might want to have emancipation. Sorry, my dear Nehru, Patel, Rai.

Gandhi Park isn't as tidy as we think of.

It is about two-hectare land. It has no flourishing flowers or green pastures. It is a dirty, foul-smelling dumping yard. However, my people come to this park in the evening to spend their leisure time or for a walk.

I was really happy to see them through my spectacles, though my glasses were a bit condensed. I dwelled for a long time in here. I could see some people are visiting the park regularly and some of them every so often.

Children came up to me and scanned me and asked some questions about me to their parents.

'Papa, who is this guy?'

The answer usually was like this,

'This guy was a freedom fighter.'

'Was he, oh? What is his name?' Again raising a question.

The answer: 'M K Gandhi.'

'MK stands for?'

'MK stands for?… Hey, don't you have any other question to ask? Do you?'

Their voice might be a bit disturbed, or if the parents have got a stick in their hands, they must wag towards them.

Most of the parents would give false account of things. Some children are eager to need to know the meaning of independence, but the elders are distorting them.

The Municipal authorities did not have a look around in the park. They did not have time. Politicians have no time to serve the people.

Then what are they doing?

They are not learning how to serve the country.

Political infrastructure is manufacturing tricky and skilled thieves instead of good and humane ones. Some are peculating money from public funds; some of them earnestly forget the duty and wander aimlessly. I could see all are running after money. You should do your duty properly or else the next generation will curse you.

My people would lose the faith on politics. Sometimes I had thought that if Godse had not shot me, I could have changed the fate of my nation. But that was my fate. I had retired half way, an unfinished journey. The numbness in my body had been deteriorating as time elapses. How could I stop this? My mind had been arousing vague compassion that incited me now and then.

I am in a position where I am surrounded with three BARs in three positions in a small radius. One bar was opposite to me, some fifty meters away across the narrowed road that stretched to the polluted air ingloriously. Regardless of colour, age, and social status my people were consuming alcohol, including the under-aged youth. There was no string attached. There was no age verification. There were no rules and regulations. I was against alcoholism, but who cared about that. They got intoxicated and puked all over the road. The second one was on the right side of me, that is, far right side; another one was on the left side of me. There was only one difference according to the facility they were providing to the consumer, the number of stars. It might have a slight variation, five-star, three-star, and two-star bars. The utmost outcome must certainly be the ruin of the new generation. The smell of the alcohol makes me feel suffocated.

The church bell was chiming far away, which means the time is seven o'clock in the morning. There is a clock tower near the bar erected in gothic style by the British, but the black palms of the clock have not been moved after India's independence. Some numbers had been missed as the clock only had 12, 4, and 9. It shows twelve o' clock exactly for more than sixty years, but the pendulum has been oscillating making a creaking sound.

By midday, I nearly slipped into a nap, because the sun was very hot. It made me really tired. Soon someone woke me up with a raucous voice. It was none other than the crow, a usual visitor. How dare he was sitting on my shaved head. His small spongy feet and his bill made me feel ticklish. His belly was very soft. He started to tidy up his black, thick plumage with his beak. After that he made a hoarse voice, which left my ears trembling.

'Go away. You are sitting on my head,' I cried out. He did not notice. He might also know that carrying a walking stick was worthless. Again a husky voice and he made himself comfortable.

'What is that?' I asked myself. Some hot stuff was flowing from my head to nose, and it blanketed my spectacles I could barely see through anything, and it smelled horribly.

'Oh, bird, you defecated on my head. Do you think that I am a public toilet? This is not the first time, remember. All over my body is stained with bird defecation. You contributed most of it,' I cried out.

He cocked his head and scanned my face.

He might have asked one question:

'Did you tell anything?'

'No, my friend, what is the use of complaining,' I uttered.

The crow made a raucous voice, and he wagged his tail, and then he flew away. I think he was coming only to defecate on my head.

Thunder struck across the sky. Dark cloud rolled from one side to another.

Then it started to rain.

Wind blew harshly. The palms of trees and bushes come apart.

Heavy rain washed out the dirty things from my glasses. My body started to shiver. I felt very cold. Who would help me not to drench in the rain?

My pathetic voice died out with the rain. Gandhi Park was filled with water. Human faeces were flowing down with the water. Suddenly, a pretty young woman appeared with another young man and stood beside me.

They had an umbrella held open over their head. Their dresses were drenched with water. They were arguing about something. It was about the money. The young man handed her money. The woman seemed to have agreed with him. Then they retired behind me under a big tree.

After half an hour, they came along visible to me.

The young charming black-haired woman was a prostitute.

Rarely had she appeared in the park, but now-a-days she had been coming regularly with strange men, regardless of age. She was pocketing money in an unfair way.

What made her to make money in this way? It could be poverty. Poverty engenders prostitution, and crime. Both are curse to the society.

The rain started to get weaker. Darkness was condensing before my eyes. The road and the park had been deserted. Feeble street light lit up the road. All the shops were closed. A few dogs padded across the streets. They did not have a place to lodge just like me.

Early in the morning, as the church bell tolls, a beggar appeared close to me with his Labrador.

He had a half-bottled brandy in his hand. He had been drinking it sip by sip. His name was Mo. He was in his seventies. His torn cloths had been hanging down from his waist to his naked feet. His grey-coloured long beard and moustache seemed to be sticky. His stained teeth were protruding from the thick black lips. He has something on a sack which was hanging over his right shoulder. Labrador jumped up but the leash which was attached to his collar stopped him further.

'Lo.' His harsh voice stopped the Labrador. He yapped in token of respect to his master. Slowly he licked on his master's naked feet.

'Okay enough,' Mo ordered. He stopped in that very moment.

'Good boy.' He ran his hand through his body. Then he finished the brandy, which he had reserved, and threw away the empty bottle.

'Are you all right, Mr. Gandhi?' He scanned me. 'I hope you would be all right.' After a pause, he continued, 'Wouldn't you? Yesterday, because of rain, I could not come here under the banyan tree. As you know that is my shelter, a shelter having no roof in it. Yes, I have got it but only a leafy roof. Anyway, it is better than you. Where would you go? If it rains, sun shines, even in the war, I am praying there should not be ridiculous war, but in that situation, where would you go? Tell me, I knew you did not have an answer.' Labrador yelped as he agreed with his master.

'You were also a mute spectator of all the events that is happening around you. How could you be silent, as a responsible person?' He was already intoxicated. He started to blabber on and on.

'Look, I am hungry really. I am hungry. I need to eat something, I've got some bread in my sack. Would you like to eat something? Oh, I am sorry you're just a stone sculpture. You don't have appetite as a normal man can have. That is the difference between you and me. I need food to live, but you don't have to. I like you very much. You have place in my heart. I know the value of independence, which you have given us. It is a treasure, but no one knows the value of the word.' He slowly retired to the concrete platform under the banyan tree. He pulled the rope attached to the saddle of the Labrador. The dog was forced to go with him. The dog doesn't know the sweetness of independence; he knows only the bitterness of slavery. He barked as he followed Mo in token of disrespect.

'Gandhi Jayanthi,' a day when my people are celebrating my birthday. All Indians are free on that day. It is a public holiday. People are domesticated on that particular day and enjoy their holiday by all means. In Raj Ghat in Delhi, my memorial place there will be a political gathering on all Gandhi Jayanthi day. After a long time of silence, they will disperse. They might commemorate me.

Here, in Gandhi Park, the day before Gandhi Jayanthi, I'll get a shower, a complete shower, once in a year, but not with soap and shower gel but with hard wire brush.

One tall guy, who was assigned to give me shower, set up scaffolding around me and placed himself on it. By using the wire brush, he scrubbed all over my body. I felt the pain all over my body.

You might not have seen the blood spot over my body, but I felt the pain awfully. Bird pooh and all dirtiness had been washed out. Now I felt fresh and clean. Yearly ablution was over. Now I was ready to celebrate my birthday.

The following day, early morning, politicians were presented a stage drama. Around fifty people were gathered in front of me, carrying Indian flag and lily flowers. Their leader garlanded me on my neck.

'There is a paramount importance for this auspicious day,' the leader started. 'As we know, Gandhi is the father of our nation. This very day, we should take an oath. Our life has to be converted in a way which Gandhi has shown us in which you would know the substantiality of truth, wisdom, reasonableness, and liberation. As the subtle example of being an Indian, you should have a copy of *"My Experiments with Truth,"* which has been written by Mahatma. Undoubtedly, I could say that. You must go through the book you should feel or be proud that you are an Indian. Honestly, I did not have time to go through the book.' He said with an idiotic smile and scratches his head. There was no change in the faces of those who had gathered around him. Either they would have heard this senseless speech more often or they would have agreed with him as an uneducated and silly political leader.

It is their fate, what should I say.

This system doesn't change.

The man's senseless oration went on. He forgot about the day. He would have thought that he was in an election campaign. The oration has become a rabble-rousing one. After two hours of speech, he stopped. They lay lily flowers on my feet and sang a song that ran like this:

'Raghupati raghav ragaram…' As they sing that Bhajan, my mind was cherishing on salt march to Dandi. Dandi march was a main movement for India's freedom fight. The intended purpose of this campaign was to protest against the salt tax imposed by British, which drew worldwide attention in 1930. Dandi march was started from Sabarmati ashram near Ahmedabad to the sea coast near the village of Dandi. My followers and I were singing this Bhajan to fortify ourselves to walk about 241 miles.

Labrador growled as he saw me in the early sun shine. Mo held him firmly on the rope as he scanned me amazingly.

'You look great now, Mr. Gandhi. You are clean eventually. How did it come about? Oh… Gandhi Jayanthi! You look like an old bridegroom has been garlanded. You had a shower if I am not mistaken. Yes, you had. I could not attend your birthday, but I celebrate it with a bottle of rum. Really sorry for that.' The dog yelped again as if he saw a stranger. Mo fell back somewhere with his dog. He was right. He needed to find out something to eat.

For four days, crow didn't appear. He would have thought that I am a stranger. The flowers on my feet dried. My life went on as usual: the road right in front of me was busy with moving vehicles. It looked like a snail, following one by one, it moves on endlessly. Three bars were occupied with all the time. The park was empty more often. I would love to see new faces but none comes along.

One day, I was really happy as some gypsies announced a circus show in the park for three days. They made tents in a curved shape with different types of clothing materials comprising wool, linen, and cotton. By evening, people started to appear in the park, including children. They looked at me in vehement enthusiasm. Someone touched my body with awe feeling. There were new faces everywhere. The park was packed with crowd. They drank, ate, and celebrated.

Inside the tent, the show continued with a sudden surge of excitement and they applauded. People were queuing outside the tent to hand in the ticket. The music played through the mike was a crowd-puller. Three days had elapsed quickly. The tent was deconstructed, and the people also disappeared. Again there is a painful emptiness. It dreadfully tightens my heart and feelings and my thoughts. The sky is blanketing with black clouds. I am alone here. No one is near me. My body is shaking. There is condensed darkness in front of my eyes. I close my eyes. I try myself to adjust with the situation. 'Breath slowly' I reiterate this word numerously. In my childhood days, whenever I feared I used to run to my mother and hug her, while she would tell in my ears. 'Breath slowly and concentrate on your thoughts and believe that you are not alone.' I always used my mother's manthra in this kind of situation, and it never had let me down. I have had a feeling that mother was around me and putting her hand on my cheek and using that quotation.

An ultramodern Theodolite was mounted on an observing stand. Its axis was towards me. I saw four land surveyors busy with measuring and calculating something. Their highly visible yellow jacket had been glittering in the midday sun. Engineers gathered in the middle of the park and were having a serious discussion and left a yellow mark on my feet. Something was written right above the mark, and it resembled a mathematical calculation, 120-m in blue paint, and they looked at me and a smirk appeared on their faces.

Engineers gathered their survey equipments and left the park.

The beggar was not even looking at me nowadays. He seemed to be pale.

His shaggy hairs covered his face. Knees and elbow were wrapped up with white dressing, which was smeared with bloodstain. It was a clear indication that he had met with an accident. He could barely speak and just managed to say,

'I can't drink it.' He had an alcohol bottle in his hand and tried to drink, but he could not raise his hand. He threw the bottle and it shattered.

The dog looked at him and whimpered in token of helplessness.

By the night, his shrill cry echoed in my ears. In the morning, the dog has been unleashed from his clutches. He did not have the strength to hold the rope. After sometime, few people gathered around him, and they were speaking in an inaudible voice. Government ambulance arrived to the scene and took him to hospital or… I was bracing myself to say the word. My lips shivered as I ejaculated the word… Mortuary. My eyes were filled with tears. It flowed freely down my cheek, I could not wipe off the tears, I did not want to. Salubrious wind flown from the east dried off my tears.

The night was bitter cold. I had never experienced such a chilly night in my whole life. The prostitute entered into the park through the main gate. She wasn't really walking, what she was doing then? She was crawling along the white pavement. She was really in need for help. Her labouring cries fell in my ears. She gasped for breath. Somehow she managed to get right in front of me.

'Someone, help me, please,' she cried out, pressing her tummy. Even in that darkness, I realized that she was about to give birth to a baby.

'Oh god! She is pregnant.' I said to myself. My body trembled.

'Where would she get an assistant from?' Pathetic.

I just don't want to see it. My mind has been clinging in a prayer.

She moved towards the bushy plants behind me. After a long silence, I heard a soft voice of a baby. It was crying indeed like every new born baby on the planet, a welcome cry, a distinct approval by itself that I am in the world like the first germination of a seed in any kind. It started to demand breast milk. As a mother, it was her privilege to feed the baby with breast milk.

Before dawn, she appeared right in front of me. She had her new born baby wrapped in ragged clothes. To my astonishment, she placed the baby right over my feet. I didn't have any idea what was she up to. She kissed on its forehead and walked along the pavement. I felt numbness in my whole body.

She left behind her newborn baby?

'Is anyone out there?' With might and main, I cried out for help but to no avail. To my pulsating heart, to my rigid body, to my vein carrying cold blood, to my precarious temperaments, I cursed myself. I wished I no longer exists.

By the soft rays of sunshine, the small baby started to cry. I looked at it; I presumed the baby was hungry.

The liberated animal came across the pavement. It sniffed now and then. The rope still dragging all the way, he made a bee-line towards the banyan tree and sniffed all around like a predator. I was really perplexed. Baby was still crying. The dog cocked his ears and was attentive as if he was hunting a prey. He moved towards the baby. After that he was just like a hound. It was not running; it was flying as it has got wings. His drooling long tongue protruded from his mouth. As it came closer, it started barking, and growling. He pressed his drooled mouth towards the baby. It was still crying. Within an instant, the rapacious animal stung its sharp teeth through the weak body. The little one could not have resisted his savage attack. Ragged cloth turned into blood colour, and then the dog dragged the little one amid a bushy plant. I could hear the helpless mourning from there. Now the unleashed animal was enjoying the meaning of independence. I am Gandhi. Could anyone help me from this ultimate prison, or perish me not to see this brutality? Give me a manly consideration, who cares?

Piling has started in the park some twenty metres away from me. While it was going on, some people around thirty in numbers appeared there and shouted at the workers. They were carrying a placard. They sat down beside the construction work.

An engineer appeared on the scene and cried out,

'What's the reason of your agitation?' he enquired. The engine stopped.

'This is not justifiable. Please do not make any obstruction.'

'We won't let you to obliterate Gandhi's sculpture,' one man stood up and answered.

'Look the proposed railway project is substantial for total development of our city. This is unavoidable. As an educated youth, you should know the significant changes around the world. We should do something to cope with the problem we are facing in railway. The highly demanding one the new railway line that permit the travellers easy access to the south India. Only this Gandhi sculpture make obstacle on the way.'

'Why don't you divert the railway line?' Another question.

'We have some time limit. Moreover, we can't divert it to another direction. If we do so, that has to be in civilians resident area, especially huge slums. We can't relocate them easily. This direction is most convenient for us and less labouring.'

'Whatever, the answer is we won't permit you to construct new railway line.' Voice of protest.
'Look, we are from Gandhi Samagam. We are the followers of nonviolence. If you want to construct a new line it should be in another direction, or you should have to kill us and build up on our blood and bodies.'

'You are insensible. You can't understand the things in a right way. If you are not dispersing voluntarily, you must be removed forcibly.'

Young engineer kept quiet for a long time. Mob had been carrying on with their shibboleth. As the slogan went on, the leader of the Gandhi Samagam was called for a short discussion with the engineer who was standing right side of me. What they were talking was clearly audible to me.

'What's your agenda?' Engineer asked in a calm voice. The leader looked at him surreptitiously. The engineer must understand his tricky smile. He nods in token of affirmation.

'I know you may need'. He giggled.

'Tonight, you can come to my apartment with your boys. What is your weakness? Money or ladies?'

'Both,' the leader admitted.

The followers of Gandhi Samagam had been driven off within no time. Before they walked away, they shook hands with each other and reminded not to miss out the party that night. Piling had restarted. Bulldozer rose towards the clock tower opposite to me.

Huge engine roared away, and it smashed on it with its behemoth palm, and it crushed into pieces. Dust covered all the objects, thick particles of it made feel dizzy.

I felt suffocated.

Thus it was the end of the clock tower. By evening, they stopped their work.

The event full day came to an end. In the early morning, the crow appeared and settled on my head. Surprisingly, he got his family with him, two offspring and his partner, a young crow. They pressed their soft belly on my head, and made raucous noise. Elders were feeding the offspring, and they ate it with satisfaction.

When the excavator appeared in the vicinity, they flew away somewhere. The first time, he didn't defecate on my head. At first. The huge machine hit in my arms. I lost my both arms and my walking stick. I nearly fell over, but I tried to get my balance. My both hands had been cut off, unimaginable pain spread throughout the body. Then the mammoth palm stretched towards my head. A heavy smash on my mouth, and my head rolled down under my toes I gasped for breath. My spectacles shattered. I could not see anything. There were darkness everywhere. Before I lost my consciousness, I said to myself, 'I am emancipated. I have got freedom. I am a stubborn man. I did not want to cry, I am brave, even at the verge of my death.'

'Who am I? I am Mahatma Gandhi, the father of our proud nation India.'

Blood and Caste

Iyer sped up along the Patna railway station. It was beyond his expectation. 'Ten minutes to two, hell ten minutes.' Business meeting was commenced at two in the evening. Now, the time was ten to two.

'Unreliable Indian railway service.' he murmured. He stood on the railway station for a while thinking whether to move or not.

'No point of waiting, to be haste.'

'I have got to go,' Iyer said to himself. While he got out from the railway station he looked for a taxi. But, there was none in that vicinity.

'Ten minutes. Oh! It is not easy to get over there,' he said to himself.

Unfortunately, there was no taxi.

'This is India. Only rickshaw pullers are everywhere.'

'Hey, you come over here.' He called an old man, a rickshaw puller, just close to him.

'Aap ko kidhar jana hey, sir?' he asked in Hindi.

'Hotel Taj Mahal,' Iyer responded. 'Can you make that in ten minutes? *Dus* minutes, Taj Mahal hotel. Do you understand?'

Without further question, he jumped into the rickshaw.

'Go,' he cried out. His dark eyes narrowed with uncertainty.

'Oh, old man, be quick!' He scratched his clean shaven face impatiently. 'I shall give you an extra five rupees. Make a move hastily. Time is elapsing, bastard, you animal.' His face raged at him. Old man has been gasping. His weak naked body bathed with sweat. He did not wear a shirt. The scorching sun was ruthlessly casting heat on that body. Iyer fetched one long rope which he got from the rickshaw.

'Move, bastard.' He slapped with it on his back.

'Do what I said?' The old man's feet attained its maximum. Along the corridors, through the dark slums, the rickshaw moved swiftly. After some time the rickshaw started to decelerate.

'Hey, old man, move, move.' Iyer yelled. But it was not enough to make him move. He fell over on the verge of a road. His body shivered. He asked for water, and then he became calm. The crowd gathered around the old man. Iyer slapped on his thigh impatiently.

'Who else is hardihood to pull this cart, who else?' Iyer surveyed each of them.

'Those who are daring to do that shall have pocketed a good remuneration. Come forward and do that.' There was no answer from the crowd. No one took notice on the old man. All of them were eyed on the white smart gentleman, having a black safari suit. 'Could any one answer me please?' No answer. Suddenly he handed the rope and yelled. 'Come forward and carry me to Taj Mahal.'

'I can do that, sir.' A twenty- year-old boy came forward. Then there was no question. He jumped into the cart. On the way, children were playing cricket. Some elders were washing clothes on the road, some were looking into cheap titillating magazine. They all looked amazed or darted away to save themselves from the madly running rickshaw puller. Within no time, Iyer got into the Taj Mahal. After having his meeting, he was quite satisfied. The young man was waiting for him outside the hotel.

'I won, I won,' he said repeatedly. 'I won in that auction. Now onwards the land belongs to me,' he uttered. 'By the way, I forgot to ask your name.'

'Chinnavelu,' he replied with a pleasant smile. His black hair covered his forehead. His dark eyes were anticipating something from Iyer. He handed him ten rupees. Chinnavelu overwhelmed with joy.

'Then what else you want, boy?' He pulled up the dirty trousers. He did not have a shirt to put on. He scratched his bottom and kept still for awhile, a contented smile appeared on his face.

'I want a job master, I really want,' he replied in Hindi.

'Then come with me. You will surely get a job. I won everything because of you. I could come here on time, and I have won the auction, so my hats off to your attempt. Come with me. I have got a lot of land. It is your job to flourish the terra firma. It is just like a desert. Sow the seeds of dreams on that desert, and one day you shall reap golden reality. Come, boy, come with me to Kadappa. Two days travel from Patna, a remote village.'

'Master, let me pack my things. I am coming with you.' He rushed somewhere to the slum.

Travel, sometimes Chinnavelu thought it was an endless journey. The first time he got on a train.

'What a wonderful journey!' The sight from both sides of the train was similar. Lands, like deserts. No water, no vegetation. Scorching heat. On the corner of the train, he sat down. He was thinking about his future. 'I would have to surmount lot of things before I could start,' he surmised. A surge of anxiety could not let him sit. He looked at his master surreptitiously. He was sat on far end. 'He is my master,' he said to himself proudly. Suddenly, train got into a tunnel. There was darkness everywhere. Only sound heard was the shattering of iron which could break his ears. He placed his palms on his ears and cried out.

There was a bell hanging in the middle of the paddy fields, a big one like a church bell, which was suspended on a platform, which would ring at the end of their work. Labourers would be happy to end their hard work from early morning till nightfall, so everybody would sharpen their ears to hear the bell ring. Chinnavelu, a sixty-year-old man, was assigned to ring the bell every day. He stepped in the platform and pulled the rope which was attached to the clapper. The bell tolled the sound that echoed all around and the sun dipped into the sea together. Chinnavelu cleaned and washed pickaxe and spade which have been used by the peasants. After counting it, he placed in a shed and returned.

'Is everything all right, Chinna?' Iyer his master cocked his head and enquired. He was sitting in a chair in front of his palatial house-'Indu Nivas.'-The bright light started to blaze. In that illumination, the house looked like a palace. He laid his head back on the headrest, and he closed his eyes.

'Gi ham,' Chinnavelu replied in Hindi.

'How many of them worked well?'

'All of them worked well, Saab.'

'Keep watching them; they're all wicked,' he scratched his tarnished, wrinkled face and continued, 'so you have to do a bit more work.' Iyer raised his eye brow. Chinnavelu was tired, even though he didn't reveal it out.

'What else more, master?' he replied calmly.

'Clean the courtyard and make it orderly. Indu would come within two days, before that you could be able to do this.' He smiled painfully and answered, 'Yes, master.'

He started his work again. When he finished, it was almost midnight. Moon's lovely rays brushed all objects. Stars came outside from the black clouds. His hands shivered. His mouth dried out. He washed off his body and went into his small hovel which was erected on the back courtyard. Forty years have been passed. Still Chinnavelu remembered the day he left Patna. On the arrival, he was gifted a pot, an earthen one, in which he had been served food. That was what he had got.

Chinnavelu remembered all these. Since then, he did not have rest. He worked away, and he kept his word. The deserted land became flourished. But his life never has been... Now he is on sixty-years of age. He lay down on the floor. It was early morning. There was hardly two hours to sleep.

'We belong to Brahmin family, the supreme caste in India.' Iyer and his bands, around ten people having white smart Kurta and dhoti, sat under a banyan tree. Iyer had a green turban on his head, which means he is the leader. Villagers were gathered around the banyan tree. Three police officers were among the crowd in uniform, indicating they are on duty.

'We Brahmins are the second after Lord Krishna. You are lower caste people including these policemen.' Policemen removed their cap and smiled senselessly.

'We will decide what low caste people should do. There is no need to send your son for higher education, Kailash.'

A poor farmer was standing in front of them with worshipping attitude.

'Kailash, look you should not go for that. If you send your son for higher education, what would you get? You will spoil his future. Send him for work. He will have a bright future and can earn money as well. There is a lot of cultivated land nowadays, and we are running out of labourers.' Chinnavelu was standing adjacent to him. He was very proud of his master.

'Learning how to plough, how to use spade and pickaxe is lesser harder than studying. If you send him for higher education, you will have to spend a lot of money. How will you meet these expenses?'

'What does he want to become in future?' An old man 'Pure Blood Society Member' leant towards Kailash's head and asked him in a lower tone.

'He wants to become an engineer,' Kailash answered pleasantly.

'Hey... hey... look. His son wants to be an engineer.' A spontaneous laugh broken out. Everybody around him was laughing. 'An engineer, ha... ha…'

'Kailash, your son has no guts to become an engineer,' Iyer said. 'It needs brain meaning he must be brilliant. Look at your son's face. Can anyone imagine that he would become an engineer?' Iyer said loudly.

'No,' all of them said in one breath.

'Look, everybody is approving it. So he has a bright future to become a farmer. You should send him to Chinnavelu tomorrow morning. He will teach him first lesson. If only you would not dare to act against my adjudication. Do what I have said or you will purely lose your job. I think all of you must approve my opinion.' Suddenly villagers applauded, including police officers.

Kailash's son was on the verge of tears. 'I will go to Patna tonight. I will leave this nasty place ever. I will work hard,' Narendran said. 'If I want to be an engineer, I would be, even at the cost of my life.'

'Look, Narendran,' Iyer came closer to him and told him in a soft voice. 'If you try to flee from here, I will kill you ruthlessly, not only you but your father too, so think of it and make a better decision. We have lots of examples around us. Did you forget about Rana who was as same as your age?

He was killed, by whom?' Iyer stopped. His wrinkled face turned into horrible one. 'I am the advocate, the judge and the executioner.'

'So he has decided to come and join with me,' Iyer said to the crowd. Narendran was helpless. No one took notice on him. He cried like a child. On that very night Narendran hanged himself in a solitary place in the village, left his dreams unfulfilled. Someone said he was a coward, and others said Iyer killed him as he was attempted to run away to Patna to pursue his dreams.

The next day, all peasants were busy. They were busy with decorating 'Indu Nivas.' Following day, Indu would come with her husband Maheshwar. Iyer was very happy that his family was expecting a child. Indu was now conceived.

'Look, Padma, our house is now blessed with the benediction of Lord Krishna,' Iyer said to his wife Padma, who started knitting a sweater for their grandchild.

'You have started to make fabrics for our expected child.'

'Yes, I don't have patience to wait for anything. Winter season would set on when she delivers the child, so I am preparing some cloths for our child.' Padma continued her job.

'Our baby boy, isn't?' Padma said to him.

'Yes, our baby boy, to carry on our legacy, like our forefathers did, he would bring fame and fortune and make wealth more and more.'

The following day, Indu came along to 'Indu Nivas' ushered by servants and 'Pure blood people.' They have received her according to their customs and traditions. Maheshwar, a middle-aged man, with a pleasant clean shaven face got out from the car followed by Indu.

'My son-in-law.' Iyer embraced him. 'How was your life in London?'

'It was good, Pappa,' Maheshwar replied.

'Oh, Pappa, you have arranged a lot of stupid things,' Indu said to him impatiently.

'No, we should have more celebration.'

'This is enough,' Indu replied.

Soon they all went back into the house. Celebration with crackers and traditional dance continued on the courtyard.

The earthen pot was filled with different kinds of scrumptious food. Chinnavelu has never seen such kind of food in his life. He ate all the food and made belch in token of comfort. He lit a Beedi and came out from the hut. He looked at the dark sky. There were no stars. He emanated white smoke into the thin air.

'Could I have a cigarette?' A sweet voice came from behind him. Indu came out from darkness.

'Ji aap.' Chinnavelu threw away his Beedi. 'I am sorry meim, Saab,' he apologised.

'Sorry, what for?' I am really dying for a cigarette. Please could I have one?'

'I… I don't have one,' he replied.

'Pappa, won't let me smoke, a bad habit started from London. I can't stop it. I didn't bring it with me. I knew they would check my luggage. If my pappa find out something like this, he would kill me. Please could I have one?'

'I don't have cigarette. But I have got Beedi.'

'Beedi?' What is that?'

'Like cigarette. Almost long enough. I don't know the difference.'

'Anyway show me.' He handed it. 'Oh, this is an Indian thin cigarette wrapped in a tendu leaf. This might be good.' Indu lit one.

'How fantastic, better than the cigarette the fine Indian tobacco, isn't?'

'I don't know what tobacco is.' Indu laughed loudly.

The window opened wide followed by a voice calling her name.

'Fucking idiots, they never leave me alone. Always chasing me. For what? I am not a little girl. That's why I don't want to come here. Now, I am fucking pregnant. Damn it.'

'By the way, I am off now. Thanks for your Beedi, l love to have it more, see you then... Oh, sorry I forgot your name...'

'Chinnavelu,' he replied.

'What a funny name!'

Indu has gone. Chinnavelu was cherishing the bygone times when Indu was a little girl, and then in her awkward age. She fled like a butterfly. She had fallen in love with a young man. One day the man whom she loved with committed suicide. No, he was killed by my master. Because he was a low caste animal(like my master says). Then her adulthood, her marriage, and now she is pregnant. Time has been flying. Chinnavelu sighed.

Time to go to sleep.

'Early morning, I have to wake up.' He just reassured by himself. He retired into his hut. In the morning, when Chinnavelu opened his eyes, he could see Indu standing in front of him.

'Meim, Saab.' He stood on his leg.

'Don't call me like that, I don't like it. Call me Indu.' Suddenly he sneezed. He could not stop it. Indu covered her nose.

'Oh god! Go and brush your teeth.'

'I don't have one.' He went out and washed his mouth. 'This is what I am accustomed to.' A smirk appeared on his face. 'Sorry.'

'You should tell sorry to your habit, not to me. Anyway could I have a Beedi please?'

'That's in my earthen pot.'

'Where is it?'

'Over there by my pillow.'

'Oh god, how could you live in this fucking place! Is this a shelter or kennel? Are you a human or dog? Dogs are living in a more dignified manner. No furniture, no cloths you've got only an earthen pot, horrible.'

'How many pairs of dress you got?'

'Only one.'

'You are working every day. Where is the money gone? Why don't you buy another one pair of dress? Even a shirt?'

'All money is with my master. He told me he would give me all the money which I had worked for, when I go home. I trust my master.' Indu narrowed her beautiful eyes. She was thinking something.

'How long you have been working here?'

'Forty years.' Indu sighed. 'Forty years!'

'I am taking all these Beedi.' Chinnavelu nodded to that. Indu took all his Beedi.

She went into toilet and smoked three of them. After that she went straight to see Iyer.

'Where is pappa?' She asked to mother Padma. She has almost finished knitting the sweater.

'He was in here... I don't... look he is coming,' he came towards them along the hall. Indu stood on the way.

'Pappa, I need to speak to you.' She advanced towards him. 'This is absolutely ridiculous.'

'What are you speaking?' Iyer narrowed his eyes.

'I am speaking about those poor people, I mean your employees. You are doing wrong. This is purely cheating. You don't give them anything. Proper food, proper wages, nothing, I said nothing.'

'This is none of your business,' he said calmly.

'Yes, this is my business. Who are you? A dictator?'

'Indu, would you please stop it? Do you know whom you are speaking to?' Padma uttered.

'I know very well. Pappa, you are doing wrong thing. At least you must give them their wages. You have held it for years. Please give them part of it, please. I beg you. If you wish to have good health of my baby.'

Iyer's face raged with anger. 'Okay I agreed,' he shouted. He turned around and went away.

When Chinnavelu received his wages his eyes were filled with tears. He had two thousand rupees.

'Find out who gave the information to Indu about the wages, Iyer murmured in Chinnavelu's ears. 'And kill him.'

'Gi, master. I will find out and kill him.' He returned.

Chinnavelu was running to post office, which was two miles away from there. On the way, he was thinking about his family. He had never been there after he left behind them when he was twenty years of age. His mother, poor father. He was the only child they have got.

'I could not help them all these years, I did not have money with me. Now I got money. That would make my father happy. He would be proud of his son.' He could not help stopping his tears.

'Postmaster, I want to send some money to Patna,' he cried out as soon as he got in the post office.

Chinnavelu didn't know how to write, so postmaster helped him to fill up the application. He sent the whole money which he had with him. That night, he slept comfortably.

On the fifth day, postman was waiting for him near the gate.

'Are you Chinnavelu?' he questioned.

'Yes, I am,' he replied.

'You have sent money order to Patna five days ago. Haven't you?'

'Yes'

'The money order has been returned. There is no one living in this address.'

'What happened to them?'

'The postman enquired there. He could understand that. Your father had died fifteen years ago. After two years, your mother also died. She had struggled a lot since her husband's death. We are really sorry for that. Could you please sign on this paper and you can receive the exact amount of money?'

When Chinnavelu signed on the paper, his eyes were clouded with tears.

He walked towards his master. He gave him back that money.

'You can keep this money with you, master. You are the owner of this money. I am not. The people who were right to receive the money, they are no more.' He sobbed.

He put the dirty notes on his foot tips. A smirk appeared on Iyer's face.

'I sowed the seeds of dreams. I was sweating for planting the vegetation. I watered the plants throughout the day. I kept guard during the night. What have I got? Nothing,' Chinnavelu cried out. He stood on the platform, where the bell was suspended. The place was spooky. There was no wind, nor moonlight. He pulled the rope, attached to the clapper. The sound echoed every nuke and corner. Birds flew away from a tree. Darkness, everywhere. Yes, indeed!

Indu seemed to have been low in sprit. Sometimes she appeared in the window and scanned on Chinnavelu's shack. If she realized the presence of him, she would pop into his hut and ask for 'Beedi.' Sometimes she wanted to have arrack. Chinnavelu opposed not to have this stupidity at this time, but he can't resist her demands.

'In London, I didn't have any string attached. I was as free as air,' Indu said. 'I did what I wanted to. I drank just like a bee. I spent the whole night in pub with my friends. I slept with whoever I like. That was life. This is just like a prison. Yes, exactly. Bounded with some stupid believes and some stupid God and Goddess.' Indu imbibe a little arrack. 'Hurrah! My little baby is moving.' There was a sudden surge of enthusiasm on her face. She dabbed her palm on her belly. 'Oh! Baby is kicking. This is very painful. Give me some more arrack.' She handed the glass.

'You don't have to do all this,' Chinnavelu sat by her and requested. 'You are going to be a mother. Ignore the past and live in the present and believe in God. Lord Krishna will guard you all the times. You did not have to do all this in your life. We are devoted to our life. We got only one life.'

'I don't want to hear this stupidity. You're not supposed to give me advise.'

'I know you are the woman of the world. I am an ignorant devil. I don't know anything about the world. I only know how to sow seed and how to harvest.' His voice shivered. 'I know only about Kadappa.' He moved off from there. Indu had been looking at him until he disappeared into thin air.

Indu and Maheshwar stood beside the open window. They were arguing for something. Chinnavelu cocked his ears to them.

'Indu, this is not England.' Maheshwar was in a bad temper. 'You were not supposed to do all this stupidity. You would have lots of consequence.'

'I don't mind the consequences. I am ready to bear it all, and I don't want your apprisal. You understand?'

'You fool, you are pregnant now. You understand that, without being known about that you become intoxicated.'

'Yes, I am intoxicated. I like to have more drink. Have you ever tasted Indian arrack, which is very nice?' She could not stand properly.

'You are a devil, not a wife. You could not be a good mother. You are not taking care of your baby.'

'Yes, you are right. I am not taking care of my baby. I hate to be a mother, because I hate you. Let the baby die.' She laughed uncontrollably.

'You are a whore, nasty whore.' His voice raged with anger.

'What did you call me?' Indu advanced towards him indignantly.

Maheshwar pushed her off. Due to intoxication, she could not stand on her feet. She fell over the staircase. She could not hold on to the banister rail. With a shrill cry, she slipped along the staircase and ended up on the ground floor.

Chinnavelu's eyes widened. He could see that the people were rushing along the house. Some people were asking for help. Some were crying without doing anything. Within a moment, Indu was taken to the car. The car darted away into the darkness.

'Yes, she is taken to hospital.' Chinnavelu's heart pulsated wildly. He ran away towards the hospital. Darkness swept along the muddy roads. 'Lord Krishna, what happened to her? Save her from misfortune.' His mind clung in a prayer as he rushed towards the hospital.

'As she is pregnant, it is of very important matter.' A young doctor came forward and told to the crowd before her. She shrugged her shoulder, and wiped off the sweat on her forehead.

Iyer stood motionlessly; he did not know what to do next. His wife Prabha was crying, and praying simultaneously. The other people were trying to console her. Suddenly, the door of emergency department opened and a nurse ushered towards the doctor.

'Madam, she is bleeding severely. We have to do something urgently.'

'Did you inform the other gynaecologist?'

'Yes, I did'

'This is a not a big hospital. As you can see, we have limited facilities here. We can't leave her like that.'

'Transfer her to Patna.' Maheshwar asked her in a soft voice.

'Hey, mister, I thought you would be an educated man. Patna is two hundred and fifty miles away from here. How could you take her in this critical condition? She is bleeding severely due to the fall, and also premature contraction has started. We are going to take her to the operation theatre. Before that, we must do a blood transfusion.'

'Madam, her blood group is AB negative.' Another middle-aged nurse came up to there and passed the message.

'And blood pressure?'

'Critical.' The nurse whispered something in her ears.

'As you can see, there is no blood bank in this hospital. Please cooperate with us to save her life.'

'What the fucking hospital is this? If it was in London, we could get whatever we want,' Maheshwar said in a threatening voice.

'This is India, and this is a remote village mister,' the doctor replied.

'Please have your blood test done, all of yours. If it is okay we can save her.'

When Chinnavelu reached the hospital, he could see all of them sitting in a corner. They could not control their sobbing. They lost their hopes. They stopped praying. He approached Iyer.

'Master.' He cried uncontrollably.

'She is bleeding. We can't save her. We have tested our blood but, there was no cross-matching.'

Chinnavelu moved towards the emergency department. Doctors were in a helpless condition.

'Sir, can you please test mine?'

'Go ahead.' The young doctor told to one of the nurses.

'Please come with me.' One nurse came forward and accompanied him to the lab. Chinnavelu remained in the dark corner of the hospital. After some time, the report came. It said the blood group was matching with Indu's.

'Yes, we've got cross-matched group of this man.' The doctor pointed towards Chinnavelu. 'He was send by the God.'

'No, we won't allow this. Let her die than receive blood from this man,' Prabha raged. 'We are Brahmins. This guy is a low cast beast. He is black. His blood is not purified.' Most of them joined with Prabha. Young doctor looked at them amazingly.

'Do you value your daughter's life?' Doctor cried out. There was silence.

'Listen to me, according to medical ethics, I'll perform my duty. We are obliged to do that whatever you are, I know what is what, and who is who. Whatever you arguing about, we don't mind. Please come, gentleman.' He looked at Chinnavelu. He followed the doctor.

After a long time, he heard the cry of newborn baby. Chinnavelu was standing in the darkness away from the hospital. With a smiling face, he moved away.

Indu Nivas had been decorated with illuminated bulbs which were scintillating in the darkness. They were celebrating the event. All have had a smiling face. In the courtyard, different types of soft and hot drinks were served to the guests. Indu seemed to be very enthusiastic and high in spirit she just forgot what Maheshwar did to her. She is an affectionate mother now. She slowly moved up and had whisky as much as which made her happier and exuberant. Now she was intoxicated. She perspired. She wanted to dance now....

Chinnavelu had spent two weeks in the platform where the bell had been fixed. He was scared to move to Indu Nivas. He was really tired. Tired of starving. He had not eaten anything for two weeks. At last, he made up his mind. Slowly, he made a move towards Indu Nivas. He could see the illuminated palatial house from there. He moved towards the back courtyard and stood by the kitchen.

'Look, he has come, dirty bastard,' someone yelled from the darkness.

'Kill him,' the other one ejaculated. 'At last, you came here. We are expecting you.' Chinnavelu was surrounded by 'God's own people.'

'I am very hungry,' he whispered. 'Please give me some thing to eat. Then I can go somewhere. I won't come back again. Please give me some food,' he begged.

'Don't give him even a drink.' Iyer appeared there. 'Master.' He knelt down before him. 'I am hungry master. Give me something.'

'Kill this bastard. How dare you! Do you know you are a low caste dog? There are some barriers in between us. You are not supposed to encroach it. You dared to give her your unpurified blood. You've made our generations impure. Now tell me what is the difference between you and me. You deserve to be punished, and I am adjudicating that.' He kicked on his chest Chinnavelu ended up on the ground. Some got iron bar. They beat him ruthlessly, like an animal. He cried. He apologized. He prayed. No God. No almighty helped him. He cried for mercy, but that fell on the deaf ears. He felt the pain all over the body. He could smell the blood. Darkness surrounded him.

'This is a lesson for everyone, every low caste dogs. We are the only one to adjudicate the destiny of people like you.' Iyer spat at his face.

Prabha cried out for help from front courtyard. All of them rushed towards there. Indu had fallen on the floor. She was sweating profusely.

'Someone helps her to take her to hospital.' Prabha knelt down and cried out.

Young doctor came out from the emergency department. She seemed to be enervating.

'Obviously, this is a critical condition. Before she was discharged from here, she was advised not to do any labouring jobs. She should have to take bed rest. But she did not take rest. Now, she is seriously bleeding. Postpartum haemorrhage. She's very weak. To revitalize her, we need to have a blood transfusion. Where is that man who had helped us before? I need him. Go and get him as fast as possible.'

Iyer got off from the hospital and ran towards his house. His mind was clinging on a prayer. Thunder struck. Silvery colour lighting brushed all the objects.

Chinnavelu opened his eyes when an icy drop of rain fell on his cheek. He tried to stand on his feet, but he could not. He swept along the muddy way heading to his hut. Blood had been pumping from his open wound on his head. He was drenched with cold water, and blood. Somehow he managed to get into his hovel. He came in front of Lord Krishna and prayed. 'Thanks for everything. Let me ask one question, why did you give me such a pathetic life? Why did you give me a meaningless life?' He pressed his lifelong earning, the earthen pot towards his chest. 'I got only this Lord, only this pot.' He shivered.

'Chinna, I need your help, Chinna.' Iyer got into the hut. He touched his body. It was ice cold. He turned his head. No reply from him. Chinnavelu had died a long time ago. Iyer's shrill cry died away with heavy rain.

Sun Never Rises

The colour posters had tossed down from an old bicycle to the potholed road. The dilapidated red-coloured cycle creaked as it moved further up. A toothless old man was riding it. He looked as old as the cycle. The vividness of the posters was magnificently captivating as the villagers made it handy and eagerly looked at it. The piglets cocked their heads from the dumping pit of the Municipal Corporation by the road. Stray dogs poked their heads into the mob. Even buffalos in the water left behind the muddy waters in order to have a glimpse at the old man and the uncommon scene. Frolicking naked boys stopped halfway and lent their ears to the announcement made from the cycle, where an old mike set had been fixed. The village of Dindigul was mesmerized for 'The Great Indian Circus' was commencing in a few days, apparently in three days. The Great Indian Circus is the circus of circuses in southern India as it captured great attraction to the people across the country, and it is running successfully all over time to time. People were glad when they saw the posters across the village. It had the colour pictures of half-naked, beautifully slimmed Russian blonde ladies hanging from a roof attached rope upside down and showing midair acrobatic. Some bill posters near the library portrayed buffoon wearing a red cap, tight rope-walking, elephant acrobatic, and even a lady big cat tamer pointing a stick to Bengal Tigers. Chandu Kumar was really gravitated by the posters. He stood before it and scanned one by one.

'When it is going to be started?' he enquired to an old man.

'Look at the notice. It depicts everything.' The old man pointed out.

'Oh, yes, here it is on 31 March, which means Thursday. Ticket price is five rupees for school children.' When he read the latter, his face paled like an uncertainty what he wished for.

He moved across a school ground, where children were boisterously playing and the dust swirled into the windy atmosphere. Evening sun was casting its smooth rays. After a moment, sun hid itself into dark clouds. The wind blew heavily. The tiny particles of dust were carried to all quarters. Then the rain started to pour down. The pale grey roof of hovels scintillated as the thunder sent sparks every so often. Tree branches see-sawed and some of it fell apart. The white uniforms of children got drenched and it stuck into their body. As they scurried to find a place to shelter from rain, they clattered. Chandu ran faster between the narrowed slums. His bare feet were covered with dirty black water from the sewage. Human faeces were wobbling in it. He placed his old torn bag over his head. He cursed the unexpected rain in the piercing heat of summer.

'Ma, could I have five rupees?' As soon as he got into the house, he threw away his school bag and sat by the table. Water had been seeping down from his long hair to his lap. 'Ma, did you hear me? Could I have five rupees?' His mother Yeshodha, a forty-year-old dishevelled lady, appeared there with a towel and threw it towards him.

'Look, you are wet. Dry yourself,' she cried out.

'I want five rupees. Will you give me that?' As he was wiping his face, he raised his glinting deep black eyes.

'You are a twelve-year-old boy. What is the money for?'

'On Thursday, The Great Indian Circus is commencing. That very day, I want to see the show.' He unbuttoned the wet shirt.

'Circus! Look, Chandu, I don't have money to give for your extravaganza. I am working really hard in the leather factory.' She started to fold up the dry clothes which she had placed on a wooden chair. Chandu squeezed the cloths and placed it in the line.

'I know, Mama, you are labouring, but I wish I could see the circus in which a lots of wild animals and some horrific items are showcased. I saw it in the posters across the village,' he started to search for cosy cloths among them. 'My classmates would surely go to the circus.'

'Chandu, you should understand our situation. You are not like other pupils. After the death of your father, I was really in a bad situation. You were five years old at that time. I did not know how to cope up with the situation. Your father was a forest guard in Dindigul forestry. The second day on his duty, he was killed by a tiger. The nasty creature attacked him savagely. He could not make it from that horrible attack.' She tried to conceal her tears. She withdrew to scullery and prepared a hot cup of black tea. 'Now, I am living only for you, my son. Keep concentrating on your studies.'

Chandu imbibed and looked at his mother and smiled a smile that reassured the caring and affection. 'I am ready to keep your trust on me,' he said to himself, looking into the drops of water seeping from a hole from the roof. He felt pain in his heart. As the darkness grew, she lit the candles which had been fixed on a piece of earthen pottery. Chandu has placed his damp notebooks upon a steel rice cooker to get it dry. After half an hour, he managed to dry it with out any damage, but his drawing book had been tarnished in exposure to rain. His favourite wild animals got discoloured and became unrecognizable. He ran his soft fingers over the dampen pages.

Chandu pulled the freshly scented blanket over his face. Even now he was commemorating the circus, the wild animals, buffoons, and the beautiful willowy Russian girls performing rope arts skilfully. They came lively before his eyes like in a transparent white screen. Breaking the midnight tranquillity, the palms of clock joined together and it chimed twelve times. It was the time for the occupants of the scullery. They were prowling across the floor and munching coconut. They squeaked in show of comfortability.

'Oh, this nasty terrible creature won't let us live. They are eating all our food stuff.' Yeshodha lit the candle and moved towards the scullery. She made sound with a thick stick on the floor. 'Go away, little rascals. I am going to hire a mousetrap from neighbourhood. I will trap all of you, and I'll kill you by drowning.' Her voice was harsh. She returned and put out the candle. 'Chandu, can you kill all those little terrible beasts. How would you do? You hapless philotherian.' She murmured before she slipped into sleep. Chandu was plainly accustomed to his mother's midnight evacuation of 'little rascals.' He couldn't help to laugh. He gazed at thick darkness. The rhythm of rain was slow and continuous, and Chandu was contemplating the circus. Soon he fell into somnolence.

The following day, 'The Great Indian Circus's green-and pink-coloured lorries loaded with commodities came along the potholed road of Dindigul. As it was heading up, anxious villagers crowded on either side of the road. Chandu was sitting at the last bench at school. Pupils were being taught the boring *mathematic lessons.* Padmini and Appanna, who rushed into the classroom, were gasping for breath. *'Enna aach,'* teacher asked in Tamil. They were still gasping. 'Tell me what happened?' the teacher enquired.

'Chandu, The Great Indian Circus *vanthachu,'* Padmini roared in merriment. Her naïve black eyes widened as she spoke. She perspired. Her parted long oily hair was scattered over her shoulder. She was beautiful and wise. It was Chandu who cried out first. All students stood up. There was a sudden surge of clattering among the pupils. 'Sit down. Sit down,' the teacher ordered. *'Nijam* -it is true, Chandu. They are heading to Mayura ground near the forest.' Appanna yelled. He was very lean. His eyes were swollen and had no playfulness. His black trousers were sloppy. Chandu gathered his things and ran. Following him, all students rushed pell-mell.

'Stop there. Don't go... Don't go.' Teacher's helpless voice died out.

All the roads led to Mayura ground on that evening in the small village of Dindigul. Circus tents were raised into the fresh air of Dindigul. White-and red-coloured tents were bound with the vicinity. Close to it, another big tent had been erected, and it was fortified with strong metallic structure. Iron cages had been installed into it. Thus, it was ready for the wild animals.

'When will the animals be brought in?' Chandu asked to a member of staff. He was standing by the barricade.

'Tonight,' he replied.

From a mike set, an old Tamil song was playing in a loud noise which had been fixed in a long bamboo in the middle of the field. As the dark grew up, people reverted back one by one. Chandu was the only one who remained in there. Padmini and Appanna left early. Yeshodha sped along the muddy path into Mayura ground. She heard from Padmini that Chandu had been with her in Mayura ground. She was really impatient. As she stood revealed in front of Chandu, a surprised voice from him ejected.

'Oh! I am sorry, Ma. As I was waiting to have a look at the animals, I was really unaware of the time.' He turned around.

'Do you know what the time is?' Her voice echoed in his ears.

The Great Indian Circus's first show of the day was immensely crowded. Tamil song from an old mike set was still on. Masses had to wait on the queue to hand in the ticket, Padmini and Appanna had been at the tail of the queue except Chandu.

'I have told you yesterday to come here as early as possible,' Appanna told her in a disturbed voice. 'Look, now we are at the back. I don't think we will have the tickets.'

'If we don't, we might have to wait for the next show,' Padmini returned.

'Now time is five o' clock. The next show will be at nine.' His voice shivered.

After a moment of pause, Padmini asked him. 'Where is Chandu?'

'I don't know,' he replied.

'Did you ask him to come?'

'Why should I ask him to come? He knew when the circus would start.'

'I told him last night to come. I thought he would have come.'

'Keep stay on the queue, Padmini. We will watch and enjoy the circus without him.'

'No, I am going look for him. Neither of us will watch the circus without him.'

As Padmini turned around and set off. Appanna followed her. 'I am sorry, Padmini. I couldn't help the weighty admirations that ignite in me every now and then.'

'Chandu has got the same incitement that might arouse him either. We are good friends. Never let down each other. If you had felt the same feeling which I have felt, you wouldn't have said that.'

'Okay. Okay, Padmini, I apologize for what I had done. If it did hurt you, I apologize for it. Let's go and find out him.' They marched forward.

Chandu had buried himself on a drawing book in the verandah of his house. His mother offered him a new drawing book. He could hear the loud Tamil song from the ground. The tide of his ambition didn't want to revert back. It was labouring job to concentrate on the book, in fact; however, he controlled his blazing aspiration by singing a poem and the recitation of it would let him sit in there.

'It is really surprising to see you here, Chandu.' Padmini appeared on the narrow way towards his house. 'We were expecting you on the ground. Instead, you immerse yourself on the books.' Padmini sat by him.

'I would love to come.' Chandu smiled and stood on feet.

'Then?' Appanna enquired.

'I don't have money, Padmini, and Appanna.' He looked at them helplessly. Appanna searched his pocket and drew out a five-rupee note. Padmini opened her fist as she had held coins in.

'You can go and watch. Don't expect me to come.' He scanned their faces.

'But, Chandu, we should see it together.'

'I know, but my situation is very bad, I know you are anxious. Don't worry about me. Go and enjoy. Hopefully, I could see the circus some other day.'

Padmini was hesitant to go away. 'Padmini, we will see it again and again. Now you go and enjoy.' At last, they disappeared from there.

The first show of the second day, Chandu stood at first on the queue. Gates were opened and one tallest man ushered on there. He stretched out his hand for ticket.

'Sorry, I didn't buy ticket. Could you please let me in?'

He pushed him off and engaged to collect ticket from others. Queue got bigger and bigger.

'Antha pakkathil, entha pakkathil,' (here, there), the tallest man yelled to the customers in Tamil, as they were uncertain where to go.

As the darkness built up, Chandu again came close to the tallest man and cajoled, the toughest guy who continued his job and appeared as if he was deaf.

'Intha valiye po, Amma.' (this way, lady), he cried out.

Last man on the queue had entered into the territory. 'Would you please let me in?' Chandu approached him. He didn't even notice him. He fastened the gate and padlocked it and disappeared from there. Sharp and weak trumpeting of Elephants, snarling and growling of Bengal Tigers, chattering of monkeys, grunting of chimpanzee and Chandu doesn't want to leave from there. Huge applauses of the spectators, and surging anxiety let him mooching around the circus. Ubiquitous presence of securities had been watching him. One fat guy appeared to him and asked to him to leave the territory.

'Could I see the circus?' He asked him humbly.

'It is so easy to watch it. Go and grab one ticket.' He smiled.

'I don't have money,' he said. 'My mother didn't give me money. She is a factory worker. I do know our situation, but I really couldn't help myself to watch the circus.' A shadow of pain blanketed on his face. The stranger glanced at his pale face. The innocent placid smile might have struck his heart. The fat man was contemplating something.

'What is your name?' he asked. 'Chandu,' he answered.

'I can help you, may be in a different way.' He paused. 'I don't have the authority to let you in.' He placed his huge palm on his shoulder. 'If you could provide food for wild animals, anything would worth, I mean flesh, like sparrows, rabbits. You could hand in ticket.' Chandu scanned his face. After a long pause he replied,

'No I am not a hunter.' As he turned around, he thought about the 'little rascals.' 'Hey, hey, what about the rats!' he cried out.

'Any creature having flesh would be all right,' he replied.

Chandu was anxiously waiting for the dawn. That night, he hardly slept. That night, his mother didn't wake up in the middle of the night. He didn't hear any cursing of his mother. There was no noise of evacuation by thudding the stick. 'Little rascals' didn't materialize. 'They might have been migrated to tapioca fields or to any other neighbourhoods.' He felt sad and even prayed not let them go further. He woke up early in the morning. His mother was outside the house. She had broom in her hand, and she was sweeping the dusty courtyard.

'Ma, did rats come along last night?' His unusual question surprised her.

'Is that a matter of concern? In fact, what makes you curious about it?'

'That is really a headache, isn't it?' Chandu scratched his head.' I know that has been irritating you every night. I want to resolve it out. Let me hire mousetraps from somewhere and I will trap them.'

'That is also animal, God's prettiest creation. That was your attitude towards them. Don't do any harm to them, Chandu!' She said in a sarcastic voice.

'Of course, but according to food web, it depicts feeding connection in an ecological community. Charles Darwin and his terminology also enlighten information about this food web. Ma.' Yeshodha was astonished of his comments. She was thinking about Charles and Darwin. 'Who are they?' she asked to herself.

Chandu had managed to fetch mousetraps from Padmini's house and one from Appanna's house and another from Shelvam's, a neighbourhood. He used coconut scrap as the bait and placed it in three different quarters in scullery.

As the clock was ticking away, his heart was also pulsating minutes by minutes. He sharpened his ears to get an affirmative noise from the scullery.

'Where the hell are they gone?' he asked to himself as the clock joined it's palm together.

He sighed in token of unfaith, 'I prepared delicious coconut for you. Are you not hungry? Come and have it.' He murmured.

'Are you having dream, son!' Yeshodha raised her voice in the middle of her sleep.

'No. I am all right Ma.'

'Why aren't you asleep, my son?' On the edge of her sleep, her voice slipped.

To his astonishment, in the morning, the mousetraps were all vacant. Baits were still fresh.

'They are wiser than you, Chandu.' He heard his mother's sarcastic voice from the courtyard.

'I will try again tonight, Ma. Let's see what fortune might bring tonight either. I will do it impeccably.'

That night he arranged mousetraps properly and waited for his 'little prey.' He had faith on his attempts. Night had been sweeping away. Eventually, he heard din from the scullery. As the clangour went on, he smiled pleasantly. A comfortable sigh rose from him.

'Look, I have got three mice.' The fat man laughed uncontrollably. 'You have told me that if I could have provided anything substantially flesh on it, you would let me into the circus.'

'Yes, I did, boy.' He stopped laughing and, he gasped. 'You know, I have never dreamt of it that you would dare to execute what I have told you. Anyway, it is much appreciated. Now I could imagine how enthusiastic you are to watch the circus.'

'What is going on there?' A harsh voice came from behind the tent and a baldheaded man ushered in there. He was a bit lame to his right side, so he carried a walking stick to support himself. He had grey colour moustache and swollen cheeks. His dark gleaming eyes were as similar as hawk's. He had put on white Kurta and Dhothi.

'What are you doing here, Ram? Don't you know that this is the time to give palm fronds to the elephant? He has just finished its item.' He cocked his head as the huge round of applause went on from the circus tent.

'I know Ali sahib,' the fat man bearing the name Ram stammered.

'Then go and do it. I can't bear this kind of irresponsibility from my staff.' His voice raged. 'What's the matter with this boy?' He scanned Chandu, carrying mousetraps in his hands. 'Is he all right?'

'Yes, I am all right,' Chandu interrupted. 'This man has to keep his word.'

'What word did he give to you, boy?' He narrowed his eyes. Ram stood motionless. His face paled and he perspired.

'Look, I was given word by this man. If I could trap any animals that are worth to be fed to the wild animals in the circus, he would allot for a free ticket. I had spent two sleepless nights to score on that venture. I have got three mice. Now, open the gate for me. Let me see the show. Promise has to be well kept as you know.' An unleashed laughter broke up. 'So you have got three mice to watch circus?' Titter and sarcasm on his face made him angry.

'There is no point to be mocking at me.' He flushed and registered an outlandish look.

'I really am not teasing you, boy. What have made up your mind to do this silly thing?'

'Because I don't have money to pay for the ticket.' His voice trembled.

'Ram, you have made this boy fool. Anyway, you go and keep doing what you were asked to do.'

'Okay, sahib.' He flushed, and then retired.

'Listen, boy, give me your mousetraps.' He handed it over to him. He opened it and let the little creatures out. They made weird squeaks as they scurried towards the bushy plants.

'Come on in, little boy.' He opened the gate. With a cheerful grinning face, Chandu entered into it.

'By the way, I am Mohammed Roulf Ali.' He stretched out his arm with a friendly smile. 'I am the owner of the Great Indian Circus.' Chandu gazed at him for a long time. He felt admiration, respect, and affection towards the circus owner. 'I am Chandu.' He grasped his hand and shook.

'Go straight into the circus tent. You can watch and enjoy it.' When he scampered heading to circus tent, he turned around and said mildly. 'Thank you.'

'You are most welcome, my boy. You can come any day if you wish.'

There was hardly any seat vacant in the circus hall. Chandu eventually settled himself on the corner. The air was tightened with the smell of *Beedi*. No one took notice on -*"No smoking"*-precaution board which had been blinking on either side of the circus hall. Occupants were thoroughly engrossed in the item enacted by the seductive Russian girls. It was an acrobatic performance accompanied by a mind-blowing Tamil song. The rotating table emblazoned with violet silk cloth. Upon the table stood four half naked ladies; they waved towards the crowd. This provoked uproar from the audience. Two of them sat on it, rest of them placed their hands on the head and raised their legs into the air and kept steady for minutes. Then they started to exchange the position by jumping to the other head simultaneously. No contacts had been made to the ground with their legs; it was carried out with great decisiveness, sureness, and confidence.

'Oh, this is easy,' someone among the crowd yelled.

'Amazing,' one lady uttered. After that a small iron ring was introduced into the scene. They skilfully harnessed the ring by squeezing themselves into the small ring together and danced acrobatically, which left the people's mouth wide opened. Another item was a rotating platform like a Chandelier. Girls had been hanging themselves upside down; as it was gaining speed, the ring in their hands accelerated speed either. The circulation made an awestricken experience to the viewers. A buffoon materialized on the stage and announced. 'Ladies and gentlemen, this is known as Human Chandelier. The first of it's kind in India, only in Great Indian Circus.'

Following that, a soccer playing elephant named Hippu, threw the football among the spectators. Chandu was amazed at the sight of the elephant that it had a pathetic lean body and was truly unhealthy. Its rangy legs were slender, and the nails had been removed. His duty was obviously to entertain the masses, no matter how his health or his body was. Who does care about it? Chandu closed his eyes. 'This is not an elephant. This is the shadow of an elephant,' Chandu murmured. Hippu will catch the ball with his trunk if anyone throws the ball back in any direction. He registered an impeccable performance and received huge applause. Then the Bengal Tigers Xanta and Zeus jumped through burning rings. Those two animals also had a pathetic look and, skeletal figures. Chimpanzee Totu played jazz exceptionally good, while three monkeys played guitars like a skilful artist. After prolonged hours, they significantly got exhausted; they were thirsty. But the animal tamer brandished an iron bar towards them to be calm and keep playing. People were really satisfied as they left the circus.

Chandu was in a magic land. He ran to his house to tell the story to his mother. He felt sorry for the animals; his heart ached as the pathetic figures flashed in his mind.

'Where did you get the money from, Chandu?' she questioned him. He started to tell the story.

'I haven't paid, Ma. The owner of the circus one Sahib let me see it.'

'You might have cadged him to let you in.'

'Yes, I did, because I really want to see, Ma,' he responded.

'Go and study, my son. You really have to, or else you might fail in the coming exam.'

He opened the drawing book and started painting on the sketch of an elephant. Unstoppable memories of pain which he had witnessed flash into his heart. He increased his speed of colouring. He loved to go to circus the next day also. He knew he should not have gone without his mother's permission. So he was awake till midnight concentrating on his drawing book. 'Little rascals' didn't turn up that night. It was very quiet and calm, except for the sound of the spiteful wind blowing outside.

'So as you said, you really loved it, didn't you?' Roulf Ali washed his hands. He was feeding a monkey with a banana. The monkey jumped off to a guava tree and stared at him. 'Jamal lock him in the cage, or he might disturb the people.' A man appeared there. 'Don't give him any food. I have given a banana.' The man nodded. *'One banana per day, holy shit!'*

'Tammu,' he whistled. The monkey followed him with a slight disagreement by squeaking. As he was heading up, he turned around and looked at the branches of guava, where he was before, which indicated, that he wished he wanted to be on that tree for the rest of his life. His eyes were watery. Chandu understood his disposition, and he felt affection and compassion from the profoundness of his heart towards that little creature. Tammu moved after him to the cage.

'Have they become habituated to it?'Chandu raised his eyebrow. He was in his school uniform. The midday sun was too intense.

'Certainly they are. We have trained them precisely. They are far better than human indeed.'

'But they need to be free from the iron cages. They are supposed to go back to forest, aren't they?'

'If they get out from here, they can't survive any longer.' He paused.

'Because they can't feed by themselves. They can't hunt for prey. They will certainly starve to death.'

'Those skills of hunting are innate.'

'If the inborn potentials are not put in to practice or if it had not been used from birth that becomes rigid talents.

Hunting and adaptation of environments are chosen by the environment itself.'

A lady materialized there and was carrying some clothes to a tent. Her hair and eyes were black in colour. Chandu noticed her. 'Was that her who performed last night as blonde Russia girl?' Chandu narrowed his eyes.

Roulf Ali smiled complacently. 'Yes, she was the artist who performed last night. She had coloured her hair and waxed her body. This is my business. I only know this business. Because of years of exposure to this business, I precisely know the love of Indian men towards white-skinned ladies, so I am making the most of it.'

They walked to the den. The huge layer was an incorporation of different noises, elephant eating palm fronds, flapping their ears, and rumbling very often. Monkeys squealed as a sign of disagreement.

'They meant to be set free.' Chandu said to himself.

The tigers were kept in different place where they had an added fortification with more iron barricade. It growled as they approached.

Chandu stretched his arms through the iron cage in order to touch its soft skin.

'Don't do that, boy. We never know when they turn to be dangerous. Only the tiger tamer is allowed to be in the cage for training.'

He withdrew his hand. 'I am sorry,' he said.

'Could I get a voluntary work in here?' he uttered.

'No boy, you should concentrate on your studies not on work.'

He seated himself on the front row of the seat for the first show of the day. From beginning to the end, he whistled, applauded, and roared as a wild animal. He perspired. At last he was exhausted. His bare feet have been smeared with dust. He went outside and breathed comfortably. He hadn't experienced such enthralling moments ever since.

'It was an unforgettable event, and it will cling in my mind forever,' Chandu said to Appanna and Padmini during class break. They gathered at the back seat, and he was descriptive and narrative about the circus.

'Let us go today also.' Chandu said.

'I haven't got money,' Appanna replied.

'Me either,' Padmini responded. Her small eyes narrowed with uncertainty.

'Well, if you haven't got money, I may help you with pleasure.'

'How can you!' they asked in unison.

'Come on, my friends. Get ready for the first show of the day.'

By evening, they had met up near the circus. Chandu led them to the entrance gate, where he encountered the same tall guy who had repudiated the access to the circus. When the tall man saw them, he narrowed his eyes.

'If you haven't got the ticket, don't dream of to get passed by.' He had extended his hands.

'I am sorry. We didn't buy tickets.' Chandu answered with easiness.

'Then get away from the queue,' he cried out.

'Don't be rude. Look, I have the permission to see the circus for nothing,' Chandu raged, and his voice trembled. 'Call Ram. He will describe you everything. Call him right now, or else we won't move out of our way.'

'He can't do anything in this matter. I am the manager in ticket sales department. So quit this place as quickly as possible.'

'Okay, if so, I would like to meet Ali Sahib. He had given me permission to see circus as many times as I can.'

Tall guy kept quite for a minute. His face darkened and then he smiled placidly.

'I didn't expect that you had a good relation ship with Sahib.' He unlocked the gate all of a sudden. Thus, they got access to the circus tent.

'Good god, I can't believe my eyes!' Padmini shook his hands.

'How did you manage to have a good intimacy with these circus gypsies?'

Appanna tapped on his shoulder in token of appreciation.

'Because we have no animosity that led to togetherness.' He smiled in a playful manner.

Circus tent was packed as usual. As they entered into the tent, Hippu was performing his exceptional talent. They stood in the doorway for a minute and enjoyed his caliber. Then they moved to the corner row of the seat and settled there comfortably.

'This is awesome,' Chandu praised. As Hippu nodded his head along with the tune of a Hindi song, he raised his trunk into the air. He then placed himself on a bicycle and attempted to use it, which made the crowd to cheer. Later, another new item of dance called fire dance was announced, in which skilful dancers entered the stage with fire stick and ran that ablaze stick all over their naked body. As the dancers performed it, the spectators were thoroughly engrossed in it. One of the dancers threw his weak-flamed stick outside through the open door near the den. It landed on rubbish, where there were a number of broken plastic bins. Beside it, there was a long rope by which the tent was fastened. He might not have noticed it as he was in hurry. Soon he got back on the stage for his performance. Due to windy atmosphere, the stick caught on fire. Eventually, the fire started to consume the rubbish and the broken plastic bins. Slowly, the fire started to spread to the den. Someone yelled at the sight of fire. Within minutes, the fire rapidly spread to the circus tent. Inside the tent was covered with thick smog. People cried out for help. They ran all over seeking for help. Few of them fell down on to the ground, and were injured very badly due to stampede. Chairs flew through the air. Soon the fire circulated to the top of the tent.

'Run, Chandu ... run,' Padmini yelled. Chandu stood and contemplated about something.

'Look, the den is on fire. Let's move towards it,' he cried out.

'No, let's try to get outside and make ourselves safe and sound,' Appanna roared.

'Before we do that, we have to make sure that all the animals have been rescued.'

'You are crazy, Chandu,' Appanna screamed out.

'I might be,' he responded.

Smog clouded in the tent. It made impossible to see through.

'Oh, Lord Krishna helps us.' Padmini shivered. She cried. Someone hit her down as she ran amok to save herself from the fire. Chandu helped her to stand on her feet.

'Move ... move.' Chandu was in hurry to get close to the den.

Eventually, they got close to the den between the panicking people, among the shrill cry of helpless miserable people. Animals in the cages growled as the roof of the den had already been consumed by the fire.

'Oh god! What we would do?' Appanna cried out.

As Chandu said, 'let them get rid off the cages,' he had moved into the den without further thought.

'You are putting yourself in danger,' Appanna yelled. Chandu turned around his sweaty face towards him,

'I know, Appanna, I do, but if you have still a little kindness left in your heart, please let them escape from here, my friend, or else they might burn to death. Will that make you happy?'

Appanna paused a minute thoughtfully. 'They have to be escaped from here. It would be a salvation for them for ever,' Appanna said to Padmini.

'Then go further,' Padmini responded.

Hippu had been held shackled. As Chandu approached him, he trumpeted and raised his trunk up to the air in order to get fresh air to breath. He had been trying to escape from the shackles by jumping. Chandu saw his watery eyes through the thick smog.

'Take it easy, Hippu, I am Chandu. I am your friend. I am here to set you free.' Hippu stopped his ear movements in order to grasp Chandu's voice.

'Let me free you from the shackle, Hippu.' Hippu shook his head approvingly. Chandu unhinged the shackles which had been attached with a huge iron bar.

'Now you are free. Go, Hippu, go.' Hippu raised his head and scanned him. Thick fog blanketed above his head, Hippu's trunk materialized there and slowly tapped on his unkempt hair: that was really a thankful gentle stroke from a big animal with the biggest and generous heart. Hippu ran across the den raising his trunk and dragging the chain behind him. Chandu smiled. *Live in a world free of human. I'll never meet you, my friend.* He already had choked and started fainting. 'I need to save all the animals,' he said to himself and ran to the cage where Bengal Tigers Xanta and Zeus had been kept locked. Tigers were still in the cage. Their weary eyes indicated lack of oxygen. They were panting and seemed to be sapless. As he approached them, they cocked their head and looked at him. Their eyes were kind and deep and sympathetic.

'Don't worry I'll let you go,' he said to them. They wagged their tail and growled. The cage was padlocked. He looked for something to break the lock. Finally, he managed to unlock by hitting on the padlock number of times with a piece of stone. Chandu opened the door for them to go. Xanta and Zeus jumped over the dense fog and vanished against the forest.

'Appanna,' Chandu cried out, 'where are you?'

'I am here just opposite to you?' Chandu heard Appanna's faint voice.

Chandu rushed towards his opposite side from where his voice came.

As soon as Appanna saw him, he said, 'Chandu, I have saved the chimpanzee.' His eyes were watery not because of fog but because of joy and comfort.

'What made you so happy, Appanna?' Chandu enquired as he scanned his eyes.

'After being escaped from the cage, Totu cuddled me and kissed me on my cheek. He was in tears. That made me so happy. My tears are an indication of that.'

'They are good than human beings, Appanna.' He tapped on his shoulder in token of appreciation.

'What about the monkeys?' Chandu was sweating all over, and was panting.

'Chandu, are you all right?'

'I am okay. We need to save monkeys. Come this way down.' As they moved, the roof of the den fell apart. They narrowly escaped from the fallen big pieces of iron bars.

'Tammu,'he cried out as his bare feet moved hastily across the den. There he saw Tammu was surrounded with flames. He squeaked as the fire came close to him. He was also locked with chains.

'Chandu, don't go there. We are too late.' Appanna stopped him. Chandu saw his pathetic eyes as the flames took his life off from his body. Chandu fainted. He could not stand on his feet. His face was sweating profusely. He fell over Appanna's hands safely.

The forest was dense, still and quite. Impenetrable thick vegetation made it spooky, dark, and horrific. The leaves of mammoth trees stayed still. There was no wind to obliterate the serenity of the climate. They sat on the trunk of a befallen tree, and they seemed to be exhausted, Chandu's face paled, and his eyes were dulled in uncertainty.

'Chandu, I had enough.' Appanna raised his sweaty face and looked at him. Chandu didn't say a word, as he was looking at the clear space ahead of them.

'Chandu, it is getting darker. Let's go back home,' Padmini said. 'It is nearly the end of a day since we left home.'

'We shall be moved,' Chandu said, 'Air in the middle of the forest is clear. The deceptive calmness in here is fearsome, but there is a beauty in it that always came into my dreams.'

Chandu's eyes widened as he heard the trumpet of an elephant close to the clear space ahead of them. After the shrill piercing cry of trumpet, an elephant ushered to the open space having shackles and chains around its legs.

'Hippu,' Chandu cried out. He ran up to the open space. Appanna and Padmini followed him.

Then another elephant raced to the scene and chased Hippu. The other elephant seemed to be more robust, but Hippu was very lean and smaller than the other.

'Stop, Chandu. Something is going to happen,' Appanna uttered.

Hippu turned around and stood against him giving more power to his front legs, in order to prevent any attack from his rival; at the same time, the other elephant advanced by raising his proboscis in the air making piercing trumpet. His long tusks were a weapon. As he knelt down on the ground, he sent it deep through the soil and loosened the fertile soil. Then with its huge trunk, he seized some loosen turf and showered it over his body. The soil twiddled into the air. Hippu nodded indicating he is ready for the fight.

'What is going on there?' Padmini asked. They camouflaged under thick leaves.

'This is the fight for the survival of the fittest.' Chandu responded. 'As you can see, Hippu, the circus elephant, coming from a human territory seeking shelter in the jungle, normally he would have to have a fight from his own species to determine who is fittest to be survived. Among the elephant, Hippu is considered to be a rogue elephant. Since he was considered as a rogue one, the herd of elephant would not allow him to be a member of their own herd.'

'Then what is this fight for? How did he know that Hippu is from outside of their den?' Appanna asked.

'Sense of smelling, Hippu has to be cast away from other elephant herd. There are two options for him. Either he should win or run away from him. But that is not easy as wherever he goes, he would be chased away. A decision has to made, indeed. That is the law of animal kingdom.'

The fight was already in its peak, trunk to trunk, tusk to tusk, and eye to eye. The earth was being swirled around. They fought savagely. Hippu seemed to be depleted in his strength. His mouth had fizzed out. Shackles were clinging with his movement. An unexpected attack from his rival he got a bad wound on his belly. A shrill trumpet ejected from him. His eyes widened. Hippu used his trunk to avoid more wounds on him, but he could not win in that attempt, as he had broken one of his tusks. His shackles around his legs were another barrier that prevented him from fighting. His opponent reverted back as if to restore more power for another wallop. Using the front legs, he jumped and elevated his snout to get a maximal impact. With a piercing trumpet, he pushed his tusks through Hippu's flesh. He fell over. This time he sent his huge tusks along Hippu's head. Hippu was weak enough to resist this attack as he had already been bruised all over his body. A faint growl from him was an indication of approving that he is a loser. His opponent's hard trumpet quivered the forest as he reverted back. Chandu ran as fast as he could. No sooner had he arrived there he hugged Hippu's bruised trunk.

'Hippu.' Hearing the familiar voice, Hippu tried to move around his head, but he could not do that. He raised his trunk and tapped on his head in show of affection. He gasped for breath. Blood was seeping down from his wounds. Chandu was still hugged on his trunk. The trunk fell off freely with a deep exhale of breath.

'He is dead now,' Padmini cried.

'Yes, he is,' Appanna uttered.

'Chandu, let's go home,' Appanna said.

'He had really amused all the spectators. He played soccer. He danced for the sake of us, and eventually, what fate he was waiting for, a ruthless death from his own species. The only culpable crime he did that he had been bound with human being, poisonous human. Wherever they go, they will make problem for themselves and around, even if it is animal or human itself.'

They passed the fallen tree. Chandu sent a final glimpse to Hippu, who laid motionless. His mind was clinging in the memory of his bespoken soccer. His heart ached, and he was in tears.

Thick darkness blanketed, and reddish colour across the horizon soon faded off in to a complete darkness. The pendulous mammoth creepers seemed to be more awkward looking. Crickets came out of muddy holes under the treacherous and sloppy leaves and fences and made raucous noise. Wolves had already possessed the vicinity for hunting, and they growled in a manner of predators.

'I am scared Chandu.' Padmini pressed her hand against Chandu.

'Do you have any idea in what way we came in?' Chandu gazed into the darkness.

'I am not sure. I think our way was on my left,' Appanna responded.

'No, right,' Padmini said.

'No, it was straight up,' Chandu responded.

'Are you sure?' Appanna asked.

'Yes, I am,' Chandu said assuredly. Chandu led them straight ahead. As they were advancing step by step, they were convinced that they were on right path.

'Are we on right way?' Padmini and Appanna asked in unison. Their mouth dried out. Their ice cold and sweaty body was as tangible as their pounding of the heart. The forest was still and spooky. Far away an owl hooted now and then, which reverberated the forest. The dim shadow of mightiest tree seemed to be immeasurably upright to heaven.

'Trust me,' Chandu replied.

'We shouldn't have come along here.' Padmini was about to cry.

'It was you, Chandu, who had made all this trouble,' Appanna yelled.

'I haven't had any idea, and since we had been advancing further and further, I had been thinking of the prettiest animals that we liberated a month ago. The enthusiasm never halted me anywhere. Now, I found out myself we had already in the heart of the jungle. We had been walking from dawn to dusk.'

'Why did we do this? When you asked us about the idea, we agreed just for fun. What do you think?'

'I hardly had any idea, but I am sure that was out of sympathy and empathy. I wondered about the fate of our beloved animals. I merely had a dream of witnessing an encounter of our Hippu, but it had materialized in front of our naked eyes. Eventually, he was killed. It is our presumption that we only need a shelter, a safe haven, and food, but all animals on earth also need the same to live with.'

'Whatever it is, we can't do anything in this matter of affairs.' Appanna responded.

'We are only eyeing our wellbeing, our reasons. The word *'our'* became relatively dilapidated into *'I.'*

Their bare feet were besmeared with mud. As they moved slowly glaring at the nocturnal darkness, they could hear thuds of munching.

'What is that?' Appanna asked mildly as he stopped on the way. The noise had materialized from about twenty-metres away. They stood motionless and stared at thick darkness.

'Perhaps that would be wild animals. They might have been eating the prey,' Chandu replied with a shivering voice. Padmini suppressed her sobbing. 'I want to go home.' Broken words came out between her clattering teeth.

'Will you please hold your jaw, Padmini?' Appanna was about to cry. They saw a Cheetah holding a deer on its neck as the silvery lightning splashed across the sky. The huge animal growled and crouched down the helpless deer and seized its neck in to pieces. With the blood allover its mouth, it looked like the animal directly came from the hell. Its fiery eyes now stuck on them. That unrivalled odd view sent shivers down to their spines. They felt goosebumps. They shuddered. Padmini cried out and ran away somewhere to the darkness.

'Stay calm. Don't panic,' Chandu cried out 'As long as it has its prey in possession, it will never attack. Come back, Padmini. Appanna don't run. Stay with me. Keep calm.' Chandu held him tightly along with his shirt.

'Don't run, Appanna.' He held him against his body as he was pushing Chandu off from him. Then there came a constrained noise of dragging the prey off from uninvited guest in the night with an unsatisfied growl.

'Could you hear that? He is off now with his prey.' Chandu said a voice of relief. Splashes of thunders visualised the plight. Nothing was there but some crushed bushy plants smeared with hot blood on them.

Dark sky widened and rain pattered down. Tip of the tallest tree kept steady in order to receive the grace of pattering. After a moment of quietness, storm blew relentlessly. 'Padmini might have gone this way, Chandu.' Appanna held his hand and pulled him and pointed the way. He didn't tell anything. His mind was also clouded as the way ahead of him. *'Might she fall in any misfortune?'* Rain doused them. Their teeth clacked. Thunder lit up their way often. Appanna cried out her name, but it ended up in empty tree hollows.

'What happened to our Padmini?' Appanna enquired. It was for the first time Chandu cried. He hugged Appanna's soaked body and sobbed.

'I don't know.'

'Don't worry Chandu. We will have a look around for her. Nothing will happen to her.' He tapped on him.

Since started searching for her, they found no trace of her. Rain had never withdrawn. They had lost hope as well. They moved further believing that Padmini would have taken the same route. If she had come this way she would have been in danger, as there was a big waterfall ahead of them.

'She might have fallen into this waterfall.' Chandu said to himself. That made his eyes watery. Appanna also had this thought in mind, but he did not speak. He nodded as if he approved the fact. If there is a fact indeed.

'Let us wait for the dawn,' Appanna said eventually. They finally found a shelter in a tree hollow in a big trunk of tree, where it was difficult to accommodate both of them. However, they managed to adapt with the situation. Stale of wild animals had incorporated in the humid and musty air. Water had been seeping down from a big hole above their head. Chandu ran through his ice cold palm across the oozing long hair. He could not control his shiver.

'Appanna, I am so cold,' he said mildly.

'Neither do I.'

'Can we find out her in the morning?'

'Hope for the best,' Appanna responded.

Time elapsed quickly. Somehow Appanna had tried to get some sleep, but Chandu was praying throughout the night. Sometimes, he sobbed. He placed his face between his palms and gazed to the dark, a never-ending darkness. 'All the hells and misfortunes on the face of earth had come down in this night,' he murmured.

Dawn broke over the valley and mountain; they left behind the hollows and set out for the search of Padmini. Near the waterfall Chandu found out her torn parts of dress, which she had been wearing on the very day, clung to the branches of a bushy tree. There was a steep cliff after that along the rocky sharp fields that led to the waterfall which roared down to the razor-sharp boulder caves. Chandu pressed the torn cloths to his face and cried like a child. Appanna looked at him. He was also in tears. Chandu didn't want to go from there. He had tried to jump off the waterfall. Appanna stopped him from doing that.

'I don't want to go back without her. What would I tell to her mother?'

'I don't have any idea, Chandu. It had already happened. We could not save her. There is no point to jump into the water to save her. If you do so, you are putting yourself in danger. You understand?'

Chandu did not reply. Everything around him seemed to have possessed a brumous vision.

'What we would do, Appanna'?

'Move further. There would be a boundary for this bloody forest. Let's get ourselves out from this hell.'

Chandu had kept the torn cloths of Padmini in his pocket. He recalled her innocent smile, and her jovial disposition.

'We lost her, didn't we?'

'Yes, we did,' Appanna shouted at him.

They moved further and further. It had passed midday.

'I am tired, Chandu,' Appanna said. 'I can't move any further.'

Chandu stopped and turned around. 'We have been walking on the wrong way Appanna. We are getting into the forest deeper and deeper. We can't get rid from here.'

Appanna looked at him unbelievably. 'Anyhow, we will have to walk to get the other side.' Chandu said.

'I would if I could, Chandu.' Chandu pulled him off and urged him to walk with him.

Tranquil day had come to an end. Another fearful twilight came up in the horizon.

'Before the dark, we ought to find out a safer hideout.' Chandu said.

'I can't see any tree hallows around here. Look.' Appanna pointed out to big tree creepers to the trunk of a tallest tree, which resembled a tiny hovel made up of tree leaves and branches of creepers. 'I think we would be lucky enough to spend overnight there.' He climbed in the zigzag pattern of slippery surface of creepers. Chandu was still down and looked at him; he was really perplexed by the sight of his attempt to mount.

'Appanna, enough stop there,' Chandu cried out. 'Get into the safe place there, close to your right. Come on.'

'This is quite marvelling panorama from here. Do you want to come up? Come on then. Now, I could see tips of the trees around me. The horizon is still reddish. Look there. I think that is seagull. No... no, would be pigeon, or nocturnal birds passing through the horizon. Dark forest everywhere. Fog had started to blanket the summit of mountain. Have you read about Mowgli? I want to be like him,' he cried out as he climbed up.

'You are insane, Appanna. Come down please.' As he moved up, something bit him on his neck. He felt numbness there. In the darkness, he saw red- coloured eyes against him, big like cricket balls, which had been stuck on him, and it was rolling up and down. It hissed. It was a big snake. He was held on its soft fleshy body firmly. Blood trickled from the tooth marks. His palms loosened. With a heavy roaring, he fell freely from the branches of tree. With heavy thuds of each branches, he ended up on the ground, like a sack of rugged cloths.

'Appanna, what happened to you?' Chandu rushed towards him. He placed his head on his lap. 'Appu, come on, what happened?' He let out a wussy. Smelly spume was seeping from his mouth.

'Something bit me... Chandu... go.' His voice cracked. After some short relapse and shiver, there was quietness. Chandu clasped his wound. He released his grip, and the blood was sticky and gelatinous. Chandu was on the verge of insanity. He pressed his lifeless body towards his pounding heart. Chandu heard the raucous growling of pack of wolves by his side. He jumped up to the tree. He could hear those predators munching Appanna's body, snarlingly crushing and devouring his frail body, Chandu jumped down and fetched a stick amongst the plants and brandished it against the luminous eyes.

'Don't come any closer, you predators. Get away from me,' he shouted with all his might. 'Get away...' He advanced one of the radiant eyes by him. 'Get away, please.' His words were broken. As he moved further, the herd of luminous-eyed predators dragged his body away, as they stepped back. Chandu reverted and searched for Appanna's body in the darkness, but there was no sign of his body but a pool of blood.

Eight days have passed since he had been entrapped in the forest. He had already been lean and weak. His shirt and trousers were torn and dirty. Prolonged exposure of inclemency made his skin tough and rough. His eyes have lost the glint. The merriment had lost ever since. There was no fear and hope. He ate snail and earthworms out of famish. He didn't drink anything for days. He had witnessed the decayed body of Totu, the chimpanzee, among the short and slender bushy plants. He had recognized Totu at first sight, but he had no expression on his face. He looked at him for a while and moved along. He didn't even think about Totu. 'How did he die? What was the reason behind his death? How did it happen? Out of famish or disease or any kind of misfortune?' These kinds of question would have dogged him before, but now, his mind was just like a white paper without a drop of ink on it. The pathetic view of Totu didn't cling in his mind for long. It didn't even make him rueful at all.

He sat under a tall tree and camouflaged himself to spend. The night passed, and it was twelfth day. By sunrise, he opened his eyes and looked away at the green meadows. He remained there and kept his eyes opened. He was thinking about his mother. His eye lashes didn't blink for a long time.

'My mother,' he muttered. He closed his eyes. The cherishing memory of his mother with him flashed in his mind. 'Is it possible for me to see my mother?' He asked himself. 'I don't think so. My mother is alone. She had dreams on me, but it would never materialize. I am alone here in this utter loneliness. I am weak… Ma,' he muttered. It was a clear realization of him regarding the safety and security that a mother can provide. He again slipped into a deep sleep, in which he had sweet dreams of his mother, and finally, it ended up into nothing, like a total blackout. When he opened his eyes, it was nearly nightfall. He didn't know how long he had been asleep, or it didn't bother him at all. Before he slipped into sleep for some more time, his half-closed eyes caught a glimpse of a herd of deer that ushered into the meadow having a slow pace and grazing the finest tip of grass comfortably and gulping down. As they were totally immersed in what they had been doing, a few of them cocked their head as a sense of hunch and perceived something coming out from the dense jungle. They were right. Two tigers leapt up on them. With a horrid sense of noise, they spread out and all swept out to the other side to secure themselves. The tigers had abruptly inappropriate timing to get hold on the prey, indeed; while they were running, the deer had left behind them so easily, as the tigers were very skinny and crippling. The incapacitating tigers had failed to catch up with them. It was truly an indication of inexperienced hunters. The pastures were now empty. Tigers growled out of famish. Chandu's eyes opened wide. 'Xanta and Zeus!' he exclaimed. He got up and moved ahead. A mild wry smile had materialized on his face. Chandu and the Bengal tigers were face to face now. Tigers growled as they saw him so close, 'Xanta and Zeus.' He looked into the fiery eyes of them. 'You are not good hunters. As long as you live in this wilderness, you won't be good hunters because you had been born for entertaining human and raised by the human.' His voice was shivering, his tender freckled legs shook. 'We are equally unlucky. We both are not fit for surviving. I had enough. Come on, take me a scraggy boy as your quarry. Come on... I will be happy as your sharp fangs penetrate through my tender body and then your strong claws make wounds all over my flesh. There is no added exposure of hunting me down. Come, Xanta and Zeus, take me, and let me end up this remorseful vacuous life. I sought out for oblivion and save me forever.' Chandu closed his eyes. The long fangs came out of their mouth as they growled intensely. Their lips oozed down saliva. White claws emerged out of cottony skin. They leapt on him. All of a sudden his neck squelched with a heavy blow of its claws. The long fangs seized his neck and dragged him to the forest. The glimpse of horizon was dark, a rayless dark night.

The Mist of Kashmir

'*Kashmir,* the Paradise on Earth. Yes, indeed, but there were no tourists, no new faces. Melancholic birds' sang in a soft voice from far away. The valley of Kashmir is now terrorizing the people, thunder of cannonades echoing in this beautiful land. Flakes of snow were still coming down from the heaven. I surveyed the dark sky and exhaled cigarette smoke. The weather was dark and cloudy. The distance between Srinagar and Kupwara is around eighty-five kilometres, one and half hours of journey. My psyche and sublimity had wings to fly on.

'No, the weather is not going to be graceful. The journey should not be called off even in the gawky weather.' I said to myself. I threw away the cigarette bud to the tip of my boots.

When I got in the military jeep from Srinagar military base I was really scared. Winter season had set in. Snow had covered in and around the road. So the travel might be in danger. This was not only the reason of my fear but also it is going to be my first experience as an Indian military officer, in Jammu and Kashmir, the world's most perilous military base situated in Kupwara, like other district in Jammu and Kashmir. In the winter time, infiltration from Pakistan to Kashmir would attain its peak, and we are obliged to protect our country from this possible invasion and we are doing it for long time and we will. As a Jawan in Indian military, I was really proud and also a little scared as I set out. I have got a good overview about the places where I am going to be from the books, and it was ill-famous on man slaughter.

Military jeep roared. We five of us sat on board. We kept quiet. The smell of newly stitched uniform gyrates around in the air. The jeep moved along the plain road. Either side of road and the valleys, meadows were blanketed with snows. Cascading mist caused the vision of road a bit obscure, even though young diligent driver managed to get on with the scenario. On the way, I saw some people moving along the road covered from their head to toe. On their black jacket, flakes of snow still adhered. Air was fresh, and I was really greedy to breathe over and over. Driving was in danger conspicuously. Jeep was skidding all along.

'Let's cheer up, mates,' one Punjabi who sat close to me broke the silence. Somehow, it was good for everyone to have good conversation. All smiled pleasantly.

'What's wrong with you guys? Let's speak off. Come on,' he continued. 'I am Harveender Singh.' With a compassionate smile, he grasped my hand.

'Hai, I am Farhan Islam,' I introduced myself.

'Oh, you are Muslim, aren't you? He said mildly. I nodded. 'Have you ever been to Kashmir?' he asked.

'No, this is going to be my first experience.' I responded.

'That is fine, comrade. You'll love it. I am sure of it.' He paused for a while. 'Girls are very beautiful and sexy.'

'I am,' a young man with clean-shaven face sat opposite to me cleared his throat. While he stretched his hand towards me, the driver applied the break unexpectedly. Jeep skidded on the ice and swept along up to the edge of the road. Below I could see the dark valley, tip of dark trees with snow on it, and protruding rocks in to the air. All of us cried out in terror for a moment. Pounding heartbeats reverberated in my ears. I collided my head to Harveender's as everyone else on the jeep. Driver's timely diligence saved us from a life-claiming accident.

'Hey, you idiot,' Harveender cried out. He was confused whether to use this rude language to me or to the driver. While he dabbed his forehead, he scanned me. I smiled innocently.

'This is Kashmir,' driver said, looking into the rear-view mirror, 'expect something unexpected.' No one spoke for a while. Only the roaring of jeep was heard. As the jeep wheeled past the plain road, crushing the snow it muted, and sometimes it screeched when it wheeled around potholed road. The driver steered the vehicle towards the edge of the road and turned the engine off.

'Okay, I can't drive any further without having something hot. My hands are shaking.' He hurried with gasps.

'I need it too.' Harveender said.

All of them nodded. We all got out from the jeep. I stretched out my arms and legs. I breathed cold air. The weighty scared thoughts had vanished from my heart. First, I wanted to comfort myself.

'Don't forget to take your guns with you, and do not spend long time up in here. This place is no longer safe,' Harveender said. 'I have spent around two years in various places in Jammu and Kashmir, so please take into consideration my humble request.'

I stood on the edge of the road, and unzipped my trousers. Water poured down as if pumped from a hose. Far away, dark outline of the trees bulged out in dim light. 'How beautiful it is!' I said to myself. All these beautiful territory came under fire by the combative terrorist. I clenched my fist painfully in rage. Ice-cold wind wouldn't let me stay there for some more time if

I wish to. My boots were besmeared with snow. I took off my hat and ran my fingers along my thick black hair.

They drank vodka.

'Okay, come, guys. Let's move,' driver announced while he threw away the cigarette bud. Engine roared and moved hastily. He was an expert driver nevertheless.

'Hello, driver, how long have you been here, Mr. …' I stopped half way.

'Hari Prasad,' driver completed without even moving his eyes from the road, 'two years, brother. It is quite a long time, isn't it? I know it is. I could have gone some where else, I mean in Orissa or Arunachal. I have got opportunity for a transfer, but I did not want to. Something special in here won't let me go. It might be of beautiful ladies,' he paused for a moment. 'I love this place even if it is dangerous.' He continued. 'During snowfall, our life would become more unpredictable. We might get killed by the terrorist or the terrorist might get killed by us. If we are killed, we will become the pride of our nation, or if we killed a terrorist, the result should be the same. Think about our corpse covered with an Indian flag… like a national hero. How sweet it is dying with an honorific title!'

'Would you please stop this non- sense.' the gentleman opposite to me said breathing heavily.

'Are you scared?' I asked him.

'Yes,' he answered.

'Why, brother?' Harveender said in a smooth voice.

'We are the only employees on the planet dying for our nation, and we deserve to cremate our body in such a saluted way, whoever will get such kind of heroic end.'

'Don't worry, brother.' I tapped on his shoulder. 'By the way, what is your name?'

'Vijay Vasudev,' he replied, 'I am not a coward, and I am ready to die for our country. Did you ever think about our family? They might lose their son, husband, brother, like us. How would they make both end meets if we were killed? I am sorry if I am off road. I've got only my mother. I was thinking about her. My father was a jawan in Indian army and was shot dead in Ladakh. After that my mother raised me by herself. She had struggled a lot in her life. I knew that. Knowing all the fact I experienced, I don't want to entertain my death. I want to live for her.' His eyes were filled with tears. 'It has been two years here in Kashmir.'

'As a military officer.' The fourth guy started. 'Excuse me, I did not introduce myself. I am Joseph Daniel.' He shook our hand. After a moment he continued. 'Don't be sympathetic, and empathetic. Emotion and compassion are quite unfit for a Jawan. Do not shiver your hand when you pull the trigger. As I have been doing it for a long time here in Kashmir.'

'Could you stop this fucking class, because we've been through this stupidity several times?' Hari said. 'We have got some more vodka. Let's have it.' He drove the jeep to the sideways of the road and halt there. He opened the dash board and took out Vodka and glasses.

'I can't call it off any longer.' While he was speaking, he placed the glasses on the bonnet.

He replenished the glasses and I drank quickly. Then one by one others started. Again he did top up my glass, and I drank like a fish. My body became hot. I lit a cigarette. I exhaled smoke into the air and looked at it. We left behind Qamarwari-Batamalo road, then National highway, and Mazbugh road. I sung songs. It was unforgettable moment. In the middle of our conversation, I slipped into a deep sleep.

I opened my eyes when someone tapped gently on my shoulder. Thick darkness was around me, but the whiteness of snow let the darkness a bit less condensed.

'You have had deep sleep, haven't you?' Harveender Singh asked.

'Yes,' I replied. 'Where are we?' I dismounted from the jeep.

'We are at military camp in Kupwara.' Hari answered.

'Last night, a fight with highly armoured militants claimed three lives,' Vijay explained in a shivering voice.

'Where was the fight?' I enquired.

'Handwara area, hardly thirty minutes travel from here.'

'That is not new news here. One day or another day, intrusion, open fire, blood shed, it was the situation, and it is and it will be,' Hari said.

'A never-ending battle.' I murmured.

We reverted to the camp near LoC. From the mess, we had *Chapatti and Dhal curry*, typical Indian food. I was really tired after a long and exhausting journey. As soon as I got into bed, I slept.

Early in the morning, it was a pleasant day. There was no avalanche of snow. The climate was quite and still. I reported to the captain, a middle-aged Sikh man having exuberant enthusiasm on his face. While the parade he addressed us and said the importance of military camp during winter season. A joined operation must have carried out with the police to foil all kind of intrusion. Keep watching all the movements from Pakistan-occupied Kashmir. He reminded.

My first day was un-eventful. Shouldering AK47 gun, I felt proud. To incite my enthusiasm, I reiterate the word, 'I am an Indian. I will guard my country even at the cost of my life.' This slogan was enough for a soldier to stand straight in the midst of all hurdles. By evening, as predicted, snowfall was on. It covered all objects. The panoramic view was gorges. All around the surface, on the leaves of trees, on the roads was snow. Man and machinery have been trying to clear off the road to reconstruct the transport. Even though it was a chaotic situation, I enjoyed it very much.

Second day was as same as the last day, with white colour snow everywhere. By evening, I must be very attentive. I reassured myself while patrolling, especially during nightfall. On that day, there was no snowfall at all, even though thick mist cascaded all around which caused obstruction to see through. I heard ascending footsteps, close to me. I became more cautious.

'Who is that?' Gingerly I moved across. The noise was coming from my right side. Again it came too close.

'Who the hell are you?' My voice trembled. Cold wind blew away. Again there was a whistling sound just a few metres away from me. Then the sound passed over my head.

'I don't mind who you are. Please come out or I'll shoot. I mean it.' I aimed my gun towards the direction from where the sound came. My finger slipped to the trigger, ready to pull.

'You can't do anything,' an extraordinary voice echoed in my ears. Without a second thought, I riddled the target with bullets all along. Vijay, Harveender, Hari, and Joseph joined with me.

'What did you see?' Joseph cried out.

'I didn't see anything, but I heard the voice.'

'What voice?' Harveender enquired while his gun fired up.

'A voice as same as a woman,' I uttered.

'Are you sure?' Vijay enquired.

'As clear as I hear you.' I responded.

Ammunition came to an end. We breathed heavily. We searched all around, but there was no sign.

Following day, I gave to the captain a decisive description about the incident. He asked me if I was all right to continue. I said, 'yes.'

The next night, I heard a murmuring sound from the exact place where it had been last day.

'I'll find out who ever it is, and will kill you.' I determined. The dense mist pulled me over to move further.

'Hello, Mr. Farhan.' A sweet voice addressed me just an arm stretch away.

'Hell, who are you? Yesterday, you had made a narrow escape. I won't repeat it again. I am damn sure of that.'

'You can't do anything. You can't kill me, Mr. Farhan.'

'How did you know my name?'

'I know everything.'

'You, you what is your name? Let me have a look on your face.'

Then there was no answer. My finger moved to the trigger. Raising voice stopped me.

'Do you want to kill me? Your finger is moving to the trigger.'

'How did you know that?' Something dropped from my heart. I knew it was my courage. My hands throbbed.

'You lost your courage. Your hands are shaking.'

'You are not a human, aren't you? Tell me how did you know all these.' I sweat profusely even in that cold weather.

'You are right. I am not a human. I am just a spirit. I am close to you. Now I hit on your face. Can you feel it?'

'What… what is your name?

'Heera. The Mist of Kashmir.'

I felt numbness. My eyes rotated. I breathed for air. Before I lost my consciousness, I saw strong current wiping off all cascaded mist around me. I fell down.

I opened my eyes. I was lying in a soft couch inside the camp. My comrades leant over my face. Someone gave me a glass of hot water, another one wiping my face with a soft towel.

'What happened to you, my friend?' Vijay enquired.

'I just don't know.' I looked away.

'It was Harveender who saw you lying on snow.' Joseph put his hand on my shoulder.

'I thought you died,' Harveender said.

'Please don't tell to the captain.'

'That is fine. How did it come about?' All asked in one voice.

'May be it was because of blood pressure,' I responded.

I did not want to tell the truth.

'If you feel so, you would rather consult a doctor,' advised some one.

'No, I am fine. Just leave me alone for a while.'

I never had an experience like this. I felt I was in a magic land.

Is it possible?

Does spirit exists?

With an avalanche of questions, I moved along the border. To be honest, I was really perplexed. Even though there was no snow falling, still dense mist was hanging. I just wanted to fall back from the vicinity. I held my gun firmly. But an accustomed sound stopped me further more; 'I hope you would be all right.' I didn't answer.

'I won't do any harm. No need to afraid. I am your friend.'

My mind was revolving around, what to say or what to do. I made myself comfortable.

'Where are you now?' An attentive question.

'You still don't believe me, do you?'

'As I am a soldier. I won't take anyone into consideration or you should show your face.'

'Can you feel cold?'

'Yes.'

'What about heat.'

'Of course, I do feel.'

'Then you can feel me as well.'

'How?'

'I am as cold as ice. I am faceless. I can travel with the current, but I melt down with the sun rays. I am Mist, The Mist of Kashmir.'

'You mean the mist all around me ...'

'Yes, I am.'

'No, it is impossible.'

'Yes, it is possible.'

'How?'

'If I am Heera, a seventeen-year-old girl. Once I have lived here having a lot of dreams, and passion, like every girls in my age. It is possible.'

'I was born in an orthodox Muslim family.' The sweet voice continued.

'My father was an Imam in the Mosque. As a Muslim, the women have no right to procure education, and we, the girls, might have been terminated to act according to our will. As a Muslim, you may have been aware about that, but my way of thinking was entirely different. After I finished my tenth standard. I want to join my higher education from University of Kashmir. But my father was against that decision.'

'No, it is time to get married with someone.' He said.

'No, I am only seventeen.'

'You are over-aged already.'

After two weeks, I got married with a man named Hassan Al Qura a forty-five-year-old man. My life was shattered when he was shot dead by the military near Handwara. He was a terrorist. After that incident, I had to restart my life. I don't want to be domesticated cursing my life. Instead, I wanted to occupy my mind in a different way. How many Muslim sisters have ended up their life not acquiring education, if they wished to? How many of them know the power of word? In my limited knowledge, I can do something. So I started to visit home by home and teach them as much as I can. People in the valley of Kupwara called me Mist. The Mist of Kashmir. Parda and Burkha was a barrier for them to know about the world. The Muslim community did not like that at all. One day...' soon strong current howled across. Thick mist vanished off. The word still echoed in my ears.

'One day,' I reiterated. 'What happened that day?' I asked to myself. I was really itching to hear the rest of it. I've spent more time in there. But the climate has been getting worse, so I fell back to the camp. I could not sleep in the night. I drank Vodka to have a bit rest, but I couldn't sleep. By four o' clock, I slept.

There was no subsequent event for two days. Moreover climate was an enervating one. But the succeeding day by nightfall, I had a little hope. Snowfall had stopped, but the mist was still on.

'Heera,' I called.

'You have been looking for me, haven't you?' A familiar voice came from behind me.

'Yes,' I smiled. 'Happy to see you.' I looked around to the dense mist.

'Me too,' the voice replied.

'Now, you can feel me, can't you?'

'Yes, I can. I see you either.'

'How?'

'You are hiding somewhere in the mist having an artless eyes. Your smooth body is wrapped by the black Parda, your beautiful face is also covered with black Burkha. Only your eyes could see through. Those are beautiful yes, a naïve charm girl.'

'Your imagination was nearly right. I had everything by the mercy of Allah, but Allah did not protect me when terrorist kidnapped me one day and shot me on my head.'

'You said you were kidnapped?'

'Yes, I was. One evening I was on my way home as usual after my teaching class. Along the control line, there was an unexpected attack by the militant. Their target was me. I had been taken with them. In their hideouts, I was tied with ropes.' She stopped. 'Their leader adjudicated that I was wrong because I tried to teach Muslim girls. They read out Koran and had shot me instantly. Military came up for my rescue. They killed all the militants and rescued me. This time, I narrowly escaped. Almost nine months I spent in hospital. I recovered, but my destiny was not to be murdered by someone. Again I intended to carryout with teaching. This time, my fate has been materialized. My house had been attacked by the terrorist. My father had been shot dead in front of me. I cried out. No one came out for help. How should I expect someone to help in those chaotic situations except military?

'Kill her. Kill her,' someone cried out. They were six.

'You know what you did?' They yelled. They dragged me towards my father's dead body. He was the only one I have got on earth. Still blood was gushing out from his scattered head.

'You did act against our will, against our decision,' one tall man shouted at me. All those covered their face like Burkha and put on a Kufi cap.

'Against your will? Who are you?' I shouted in a heavy breath.

'We are the followers of Allah. We'll kill those who are against Islam.'

'Procuring education was against Islam?'

'Yes, Muslim women should not acquire education. If you are educated you must devalue the power of men. This world is made up only for men. All most all the gods are men like Jesus, our prophet, Buddha, Sri Krishna, Siva. Like you woman, your fate is give birth to babies until you are exhausted. Let the world be ours, Islam. You act against that unwritten law. You deserve death. Be Allah praised.'

'So be it,' all said.

He pulled out Koran from his pocket. One of them placed knife on my throat.

'Everything accomplished.' I closed my eyes. Next moment, a bullet fond it's way through the leader's head. Blood spattered all over the wall behind him.

'Allah,' all said in a same breath. 'Indian military,' someone yelled, and fired all along, but to no avail. They have been gunned down. Blood splashed all over my body. First a military officer came into the vicinity.

'All clear,' he announced. Three soldiers accompanied him.

They found out me amongst the debris.

'Are you scared?' one of them passed through his strong hand along my shivering body. I could see the lustful glittering in his black eyes.

'You are beautiful, aren't you?' The second one took off my Burkha. It was the first time I unveiled my face in front of a strange men. My eyes were filled with tears.

'In the name of Allah, don't do it,' I begged in front of them.

'Look how beautiful she is… Look at her eyes. It is so seductive.' I could sense the motivation of their talk. I tried to get rid from their clutches. In that vein attempt, they tore up my Parda. My naked body made them like a lustful animal. One soldier put his gun into my mouth. I searched for Koran among the debris. I've got it soaked in cold blood. I pressed it against my naked chest and prayed. 'Allah, save me.'

'Don't shout. If you do not co-operate with us, we will kill you for sure.' They dragged me into the next room. In that darkness they took all my dress off and used me one by one, five hours continuously.

'Allah, help me… help me.' The only word I could say in that moment even though I did not lose holy Koran. My vagina has started bleeding in spite of this. They sucked blood from there. When they dressed up themselves again, it was nearly morning.

'Kill her.' Someone amongst them ordered. One of them placed his gun into my mouth and pulled the trigger. Blood stained Koran dropped from my hand. That was the end of Heera. The Mist of Kashmir.

I could not control my sobbing. 'Heera,' in a loving voice, I called her.

'Who are they?' I shouted.

No answer. Darkness utmost darkness was around me. My hands were shaking in surge of rage.

'I want to kill them,' I held the gun tightly. 'Heera.'

'That was none other than your four comrades.'

'Who Harveender and Vijay.…'

'Joseph and Hari,' she completed.

'Farhan, we have got one message from police.' One soldier came up to me.

'What is that?' I enquired.

'In Hanwara area, they suspect an intrusion. Heavily armed terrorists. So we have to make a move now.' He responded.

'Get ready. I am coming.'

I left Heera for a while.

'I will be right back, Heera.' I said to myself.

I mounted on the jeep. On board I have got the same company, my four comrades. They were sitting opposite to me.

My mind was still clinging in around Heera. In Hanwara, the situation was more tensed than I thought.

The terrorists surrounded a house heavily armoured. So I must be very attentive. I placed myself in an area where they were in my range so that I could easily gun them down. There were six in numbers. Inside the house, I could see in feeble light someone tiding up the hostages and placing the gun on an old Muslim man. One… two… three… aimed, fired one down. I have to be haste or will lose all hostages. I signalled my comrades to move close to the house.

I was close to the door. No, they can't anticipate that we were so close to the house. We were swept along the way to the door. The next moment, I fired up the door. The lock shattered. I held the door opened. 'Surrender or else we'll shoot you,' I yelled. No sooner had we entered the house, the guns fired up. I myself did not want to stop the firing till a bullet from the terrorist got me down, which pierced through my shoulder. All guns died off. My shoulder was bleeding. I felt the pain. Then, I lost my consciousness.

My mind was awakened when I was hoisted to an ambulance. The paramedical staff fixed oxygen masks on my mouth. I started breathing cold air.

'No, we are taking him to Srinagar Military Hospital. His condition is stable, but I am not quite sure about his left hand. The shoulder has totally shattered.' Medical staff must be answering to the captain.

'He might undergo a surgery. Okay then, we'll keep in touch with you. Bye.'

The door closed.

Vehicle moved.

I slipped into a sleep. I don't know how long I have been in deep sedation.

I opened my eyes.

Paramedical staffs were reading book beside me. One was *'Dark Winter,'* and another was *'Roses Are Red.'*

'Are you all right'? The short guy looked at me and enquired. I nodded. He closed the book and threw it into a corner. He might have been exhausted.

Then he turned on the radio in which news bulletin was on from All India Radio. The news ran like this in a male voice.

'Today an intrusion attempt foiled by Military in LoC near Hanwara area Jammu and Kashmir. Terrorist were heavily armoured. Fortunately, military personnel gunned down six militants. Sadly, we lost four jawans, Harveender Singh from Punjab, Vijay Vasudev from Tamilnadu, Hari Prasad from Delhi, and Joseph Daniel from Goa. The terrorists struck back. Around half an hour, the fight went on. All hostages are rescued. This is the third time Pakistan...' the volume weakened.

'Can I have a glass of water?' I asked.

'Yes, of course.' The tall guy offered me a glass of water. I drank it and laid down on the crèches. My eyes were stuck on the white roof of the ambulance. The colour was just like mist. I felt coldness all over my body. That moment, yes, I felt it.

'Heera,' my dried lips murmured. 'The Mist of Kashmir.'